A Piece of Forever

A Piece of Forever

by

Laurel Dee Gugler

James Lorimer & Company Ltd., Publishers
Toronto

James Lorimer & Company Ltd. acknowledges the support of the Ontario Arts Council. We acknowledge the support of the Government of Canada through the Book Publishing Industry Development Program (BPIDP) for our publishing activities. We acknowledge the support of the Canada Council for the Arts for our publishing program. We acknowledge the support of the Government of Ontario through the Ontario Media Development Corporation's Ontario Book Initiative.

Cover design: Meghan Collins

The Canada Council | Le Conseil des Arts
for the Arts | du Canada

ONTARIO ARTS COUNCIL
CONSEIL DES ARTS DE L'ONTARIO

Library and Archives Canada Cataloguing in Publication

Gugler, Laurel Dee
    A piece of forever / Laurel Dee Gugler.

(Streetlights)
ISBN 978-1-55277-026-9

    1. Mennonites — Juvenile fiction. I. Title. II. Series.
PS8563.U44P53 2008   jC813'.54   C2008-904681-1

James Lorimer & Company Ltd.,
Publishers
317 Adelaide Street West
Suite #1002
Toronto, Ontario, M5V 1P9
www.lorimer.ca

Distributed in the
United States by:
Orca Book Publishers
P.O. Box 468
Custer, WA U.S.A.
98240-0468

Printed and bound in Canada.

For all children everywhere. May you find the seeds of peace in each piece of forever, and may these seeds grow through stone.

L.D.G.

1

Bye-Bye Bird

"How did the bird get dead?" My little brother Daniel squats beside the stiff bird. Its legs stick up, toes curled, and its eyes are sunken. Daniel's face is all scrunched up and sad. Daniel loves every single kind of animal, even bugs and spiders.

"I don't know how the bird died, Daniel. Maybe it fell from the tree. It looks too tiny to fly." The bird is already smelly, a rotting smell. *Phew!* Tiny insects crawl all over it.

"Let's do a funer-o." Daniel is five and still can't say his l's. I sure hope he learns before he starts school next year. He doesn't go yet because we don't have a kindergarten at Prairie View Elementary. Daniel is small for his age, and cross-eyed.

Sometimes kids tease him. It makes me boiling mad.

"Daniel, we can't have a funeral now because I gotta go to school. I don't want to be late."

"But we have to have a *funer-o*, wike when Tante O-ga got dead."

"Well, Tante Olga didn't have a funeral early in the morning before school. We'll have a funeral when I get home."

"But what should I do with the bird?"

I sigh, changing my mind about putting off the funeral. If I leave now, goodness knows what Daniel will do with the bird. What if he carries it around all day?

"Okay, we'll bury it now, but it will have to be a short funeral." I find a strong, pointy branch for digging. "We'll bury it under Grandmother Oak, so she can sort of watch over it."

Grandmother Oak is my thinking tree, where I go when I want to be alone. To me, Grandmother Oak feels almost like a person. She has a comfy-cozy place to sit, sort of like a lap, and branches that reach around like arms. My real grandma died when I was two. Mamma says I used to sit on her lap.

"But we need a coffin-box," says Daniel. "Tante O-ga had a coffin-box."

"Daniel, I don't have time to find a box. Anyway, it's much better without a coffin, because the bird will soon mix right into the ground ... and ... help the flowers grow."

"But the bird is *dead*. It *can't* hewp the fwowers grow."

"Well, the bird's body has ... um ... minerals ... and stuff that make it good for growing flowers. It would take much longer for the bird to mix into the ground if it were in a box." I start digging.

"Oh." Daniel's forehead scrunches and his eyes move back and forth behind his dark-rimmed glasses. His eyes do that when he's thinking. "Didn't Tante O-ga hewp the fwowers grow?"

"It took a lot longer because of the coffin."

The ground is hard and the digging takes forever. I'm glad I left the house early. I wanted to get to school early so I'd have time with my friends. It's not like the beginning of last year when I came just before the bell, so I wouldn't have to talk to other kids. Last year, at first, my only friend was Sandra. She is a Mennonite like me.

Finally, the hole is big enough. Daniel goes to the bird. "Daniel, don't pick it up. I'll get a hanky …" Oh no! It's too late. He has already picked it up with his *bare hands*. He doesn't know about getting germs from dead animals. He only wants to take care of the little bird, even though it's dead. He walks slowly, cupping the bird in his hands. He puts it gently into the hole.

"Bye-bye, bird." He sniffles a bit and wipes his sleeve across his nose. I put my arm around him.

"What kind of bird is it?" he asks.

"A sparrow."

"Oh." Daniel's eyes move back and forth. I wonder what's going on in his head. "*God sees the witto sparrow faw.*" He sings his Sunday School song about the little sparrow falling. "Rose, did God see *this* sparrow faw?"

"Yeah, I guess so."

"Then why didn't God pick him up ... and put him back on the tree?" A good question. What good is seeing a sparrow fall if you don't do anything about it? If I ask Mamma stuff like that, she says it's irreverent, or even blasphemy. Blasphemy is when you say, or even think, something wrong about God or the Bible. I don't want to think anything wrong about God. I just want to figure out the why of things.

"I don't know why God didn't put the sparrow back onto the tree, Daniel."

Daniel stares at the bird, his body hunched in a sad little ball. But I have the jittery-twitters because I'm afraid I'll be late for school. And what if I smell like dead bird when I get there?

"Daniel, I have to go to school. It's time to put dirt over the bird."

"But, Rose, did the bird go to heaven?"

"We can talk about it more when I come home."

"Okay, Rose." He looks at the sparrow a couple of seconds longer, then pats dirt over it.

"We'll go wash our hands, Daniel, and then I

have to run. Find a stone to put over the spot."

"But can the fwowers push through the stone?"

"Flowers?"

"You *said*, the sparrow would hewp some *fwowers* grow."

"Um ... find a small stone that flowers can grow around." I don't know if I should have said that, but I had to think of something quick. Maybe he thinks flowers will grow right away, without seeds or anything. What if he comes to check every single day?

We wash our hands. As I dash off to school, I notice a straggly yellow cat. It has wild eyes and zips away when it sees me. It's not like our cat, Stinker, who likes being with people. I guess this new cat is a stray. I've never seen it before.

2

Uncle Sam Wants You!

Mr. Foster, our stern-faced teacher, glares at me as I slip into my seat after the bell. "Good deportment requires *punctuality*." Such big words he uses. "What do you have to say for yourself?"

What should I say? I had to go to a funer-o? I had to bury a bird? My tongue is stuck. I say nothing at all. I feel myself blush. He lets it go, maybe because I haven't been late before. "See that it doesn't happen again."

At recess Cindy comes to Sandra and me. "How come you were late?" she asks. Cindy got to be my friend last year. She helped me practice softball till I got good at it.

I tell Cindy and Sandra about the dead bird

and the funeral. "There were tiny bugs crawling over the bird and it was starting to get smelly." I can't resist telling them that part.

"Oooh yuck!" says Cindy.

Sandra's eyes open wide. "You came to school full of *germs?*" She backs away.

"I didn't even touch the bird. Daniel put it into the hole I dug. And, even so, I washed my hands a gazillion times."

The day humdrums along. As usual, we play softball. As usual, Sandra is chosen last, and I'm chosen near the beginning — not like the start of last year, when I was chosen second to the last. As usual, Judy says something dumb about Sandra's dress being too long. *When you gonna stop wearing old-lady dresses?* I finally convinced Mamma to let me wear jeans, by telling her it wasn't ladylike to wear dresses when playing ball. Not that I want to be ladylike, but it was the only way to convince Mamma.

Back in the schoolroom, during last period, things get awful.

Mr. Foster holds up a poster that says, "*Uncle*

Sam Wants YOU!" Uncle Sam's eyes blaze from the poster. He is a skinny guy with a sharp nose and a long, bony finger pointing out of the poster. It looks like he's pointing at me. He's wearing a tall hat and his clothes are red, white, and blue, like our United States flag. "What does Uncle Sam symbolize?" asks Mr. Foster.

"He doesn't look like my uncle," I whisper to Cindy.

"Rose," says Mr. Foster in a fierce voice, "if you have something to say, speak loudly enough for us all to hear."

I can't look at Mr. Foster's face. "He doesn't look like my uncle," I say in a small voice. "It was a *joke*."

"Rose! This is *not* a joking matter. Uncle Sam stands for our United States ..." He answers his own question. His voice gets even louder. "... and, though not an actual person, in a very real sense, *he is your uncle!*"

The other kids snicker, but then it gets real quiet. *What did I say that was so horrible? I was only joking.* Mr. Foster continues, "The United States and its armed forces are here for the protection of *you*, Rose, and all of us in this room, in this state, in this country." Shame spreads through me, and I don't even know what I said that was so terrible. I don't dare look up, but I can feel everyone staring at me.

Finally Mr. Foster talks again, his voice softer now, and I dare to breathe. I can hear shuffly, whispery sounds as if the whole room has started breathing again. "This poster is asking men and women to join up — to enlist in the armed forces." Judy smirks at me. Mr. Foster continues, "Why do you think that men and women are being recruited now, in 1956, after World War II and the Korean War are over?" Lots of kids put up their hands.

"Tom?"

"'Cause we ..."

"Speak correctly, Tom."

"Because we gotta ... I mean we have to have a strong army in case there is another war." Then Tom adds proudly, "My papa fought against Hitler."

"Good! And yes, it is important to maintain

strong military reinforcements for our national security." There he goes with his big words again. "I also fought against the Germans."

My family is German. Mamma and Papa speak German. That doesn't mean they like the horrible stuff that Hitler did during World War II, like killing millions of Jews. Anyway, on top of the horribly embarrassing Uncle Sam thing, I don't know what to think about this recruitment business, because my family and my church believe war is not a way to solve problems between countries. I look at Sandra and see that she feels bad too. She is staring at her desk. She looks confused.

Kids are waving their hands like mad.

"Yes, Cindy," says Mr. Foster.

"My papa fought against Hitler, too. He was injured. And my brother, Gerald, just signed up."

"Good. We owe your father and your brother a big debt of gratitude."

Cindy beams.

Judy is also waving her hand like mad. She has a proud, smirky smile.

"No need for all that arm-waving, Judy, but what is it?"

"*My* papa fought in the Korean War ... and my uncle *died* in the Korean War." Mr. Foster turns away for a few seconds and Judy looks confused. I guess she was expecting him to say something wonderful about her papa and her uncle.

"Thank you, Judy. My son fought in the Korean War too." His voice is quieter than usual, and even a little wobbly. "But no more war talk right now."

He turns and writes 'Current Events Projects' on the blackboard. Even after he is finished writing, he doesn't turn around for a long time. Kids look at each other with wondering faces. When he finally turns around, he looks strange. He doesn't have his usual sure-of-everything expression. "Instead of telling you about your current events projects right now, I'll wait until tomorrow. We'll have silent reading for the last ten minutes before going home." We *never* have silent reading at this time of the day.

After school, Judy sidles up to me where I'm

standing in the schoolyard with Cindy and Sandra. She says in a high, nasty voice, "He doesn't look like my uncle." Judy was horrible to me last year, until I got spunky and learned to stand up to her. This year she has mostly ignored me. But she still tries to bug me sometimes when she thinks others might join her.

I look her in the eye. "I was only joking."

"My papa says you're not patriotic. You don't even love our country."

"I do *so* love our country."

Just then, here he comes. Judy's papa rumbles into the schoolyard in a rickety, red pickup. He blasts the horn. "Get over here!" he shouts out the window.

Judy runs to the pickup, tossing her head as if she doesn't even care that her papa is being so nasty. But I notice her face turning red.

Judy's papa sure isn't very nice. I wonder if that's why she's so nasty sometimes.

"Anyway," I say again to Cindy and Sandra, "what I said about Uncle Sam was a *joke*."

Cindy stares at me. "My papa agrees with

Judy's papa ... ah ... that you Mennonites aren't patriotic, because you don't fight to protect our country." She talks quietly — not nasty — but turns away as if she doesn't want to look at me. My eyes sting. Only Sandra walks beside me. Sandra is my forever friend. So why do I feel almost mad at her sometimes?

When I get home, Daniel pops out from the space under the porch steps. That's his cozy place, where he likes to go sometimes. "Come see the stone I found," he says.

"Stone?"

"For the *bird*."

"Oh, yeah."

"You *forgot?*"

His voice makes it sound like I did the biggest crime ever. My head is too full of other worries. *You're not patriotic. You don't fight to protect our country.* How could Cindy walk away from me?

Daniel takes my hand and pulls me to the place where we buried the bird. A pathetic, lop-sided stone sits over the spot.

That's the stupidest-looking stone I ever saw. But

seeing Daniel's sad face staring up at me, I say, "Um ... good stone." I know I'm not obeying the thou-shalt-not-lie rule. But I'm obeying the do-unto-others rule, the one about treating people the way you want to be treated. I sure wish Judy and Cindy had obeyed the do-unto-others rule.

Daniel is still hanging onto my hand. He looks up at me with big eyes. "Wiw the fwowers grow around the stone?"

I think quickly. "In the springtime we'll plant seeds around the stone. The dead sparrow will help the seeds grow into flowers. Ah ... I gotta go, Daniel." I need to go to my thinking place in Grandmother Oak's branches.

"But, Rose, did the sparrow go to heaven to be with God, wike they said about Tante O-ga at her funer-o?" He must have been worrying about the bird all day.

"Ro-o-ose." Mamma is calling. I guess I can forget about going to Grandmother Oak.

I think about Daniel's question for a bit, even though I'll be in trouble with Mamma. "I don't know, but if I were in charge of heaven, I'd make sure that there were lots and lots of birds." Maybe thinking about being in charge of heaven is a big, fat blasphemy.

"And they'd fwy around God's head?" I laugh, and Daniel giggles a jingly little giggle. Where does he get his ideas? He flaps his arms and zooms about. "I'm a bird." I'm glad he feels better.

"*Rose!*" Mamma's voice is louder. "Go gather the eggs *right now!*"

As I head off to the henhouse, I see the wild-eyed cat again. This time I get a better look. He is a boy cat. He is so skinny. I can see his ribs. Like last time, as soon as he notices me, he zooms behind the barn. After chores, I put a bowl of milk behind the barn. When I check later, the milk is gone.

3

Current Events

As I walk into the classroom the next day, I glance at Cindy. She seems embarrassed. She looks away.

Mr. Foster is back to his big, booming self. He's wearing his usual clothes — a stiff, white shirt and dark pants that are perfectly creased down the front. "All stand for the Pledge of Allegiance." We stand with our hands over our hearts.

"*I pledge allegiance to the flag, of the United States of America ...*"

"*Tom!*" yells Mr. Foster. "Erect posture." Remembering yesterday, I can't help being glad I'm not the only one who gets yelled at, though I probably shouldn't be glad when someone gets into trouble. "*And*, it should go without saying, face the flag. You *will* do the pledge properly." Tom's face gets beet red. The classroom gets completely quiet. This really *is* almost like yesterday. "Now, start again."

After the Pledge of Allegiance, Mr. Foster says, "The flag is a symbol of our great country, where we enjoy freedom and opportunity. In respecting the flag, we also respect those who bravely fought and ... died." He turns his face away for just a second.

Sitting across from me, Judy whispers, "What war did *your* papa fight in?" I pretend I don't hear. She whispers louder, "I said, what war ..."

"*Quiet!*" thunders Mr. Foster.

Judy knows my family doesn't believe in going to war.

At recess Judy says, "Hey, Rose, you didn't answer me. What war did *your* papa fight in?"

I don't know what to say, but I look Judy straight in the eye. Other kids are staring. Finally I say, "My family doesn't believe war is the right way to solve things."

"You think you know what's right and we don't?" yells Judy. "You think you're better than we are? Well, my papa fought for our country. *Your* papa is just a yellow-bellied *chicken*, that's what!"

"My papa worked for our country too — only in a different way. He went to ..." I try to remember what Papa told me. Something about a place where he did stuff for the government. "He went to ... to CPS camp where ..."

"Your papa went to *camp?*"

My face is hotter than our basement furnace.

Judy rants on. "All the brave folks were *fighting*, getting wounded and *killed*. Cindy's papa fought against Hitler." Judy moves to stand beside Cindy. "And *my* papa fought in the Korean War. And your papa went to *camp!*"

Everybody laughs.

Now Judy really gets going. "Did your papa do some nice crafts at camp? Did he make a pretty macaroni necklace for our country?"

This is terrible! It feels so awful I almost can't think, but still I notice things, like ...

... Sandra shrinking more than usual.

... Cindy looking at me — frowning.

... All the kids standing in a circle around us, watching.

I don't know what to say, but just keep telling myself, *Do not back down.* I hear my Aunt Bette's words: *Spunk doesn't hang its head.* I glare at Judy. I'm tired of this. I put up with her stupid bullying most of last year, until I finally stood up to her. And now ... somehow she's at it again. Even Cindy seems to be turning against me. I can't stand it.

Judy walks towards me, and puts her stupid face an inch from mine. But before she says anything, I yell, "*Well, my papa didn't kill people like yours did!*" I'm almost crying. I quickly turn away, but Judy sees.

"Cry baby," she taunts.

The bell rings and I walk towards the schoolhouse. Alone.

Cindy hurries on ahead, not looking at me. Then Sandra comes to walk beside me. And suddenly I almost hate her, though I can't figure out exactly why. Maybe ... I don't know ... maybe because she always wants to do stuff in the same old way. She still wears those dresses that are way too long. She is so ... unspunky. But that's the way I used to be. And I guess her mamma still *makes* her wear those dresses. I know I'm not being fair.

"Current events projects," says Mr. Foster. "Each of you will research some event that is going on in the world right now, either here or far away. It is important to know what is going on now, because it is part of the bigger picture. What is happening now will become part of our history and our future."

Hmmm, that's kind of like a thought that popped into my head once when I was with Grandmother Oak. *Each moment is a piece of forever.*

Mr. Foster continues, "Choose something that interests you. Our *Current Events Newsletter* may help." Everybody in our class gets a copy of this small newspaper that tells about stuff that is happening all over the world.

Judy raises her hand. "How about the army

27

recruitment that is going on right here ... and all over the United States?"

"That would be excellent."

Judy smirks at me, her head high and haughty.

"You will work in pairs or in groups of three." Before I can stop myself, I glance at Cindy again. She is looking at other kids, obviously ignoring me. This feels as bad as choosing up sides for softball did last year, back when I was almost the last one chosen. Nobody will want to work with me — not after what happened. Nobody except Sandra. I look at her and, sure enough, she is staring at me, a question in her eyes. I look down and doodle in my workbook. I don't want to think about this right now.

Mr. Foster's voice drones on. "Your project will have three parts, a written component ..."

"What's a 'component?'" asks Tom.

"Consult your dictionary."

I'm only half listening to Mr. Foster, because my head is so busy with other stuff. How can Cindy be my friend and then, all at once, not be?

"Secondly," Mr. Foster says, "you will prepare

an oral report. Thirdly, your projects will include an artistic component. The artistic part could be pictures you make, or a poster." Sandra lifts her head. She's even smiling a little. She's a good artist. "You could even perform music, or a short drama."

After school Sandra asks, "Should we work together on the current events project?" She sounds worried.

"Yeah." I feel kind of bad that I ignored her earlier. "My head is a jumble right now. Can we talk about this later?"

"Yeah."

Cindy walks past me and goes to Judy. They giggle and talk, even though Cindy didn't even used to like Judy that much. My belly boils. After Judy leaves, I march over to Cindy, though my heart is thumpity-bumping. In my head I say, *Do you have to be so snooty, just because my family doesn't believe in war?* Out loud I say, "Just because my family doesn't believe in going to war, doesn't mean we ... can't be friends."

She looks at me. Her expression is not exactly

nasty, but she sure isn't smiling. She scuffles her feet in the dirt, looking down. "My papa says that war is *absolutely necessary*. He says that you are ... uh ... protected along with everyone else, and the whole time you are safe and ... um ... sancti ... sanctimonious."

"*Sanctimonious?*" The word almost makes me laugh.

"That means, thinking you are so ... uh ... holy, and better than others."

Holy? Better than others? "I don't think that at all. It seems like you don't want to be my friend because of something your papa thinks."

"I think it too."

"Well, we don't have to agree about every single thing to be friends." Cindy looks confused. "Real friends stick together," I say.

Again she looks down. "I gotta go," she says, and walks away.

Who needs her anyway? But I have a big lump in my throat.

4

War Questions

I rest in the branches of Grandmother Oak. What if Mr. Foster and the kids are right? Maybe it's just stupid not to go to war. If nobody fought Hitler, would he have taken over the whole world? A country has to protect itself, like a kid has to protect herself. What if I gave Judy just one good whack on the jaw? Maybe then she'd leave me alone for good. Of course I did push her down once last year. Then I felt guilty forever after. Anyway, I can't whack Judy on the jaw because I just told the kids that we don't believe in fighting. So now I'm stuck. And now even Cindy is turning against me. That hurts most of all. "What should I do, Grandmother?" She murmurs, but I can't figure out any real words — just whisper-rippling sounds. "You're no help." Suddenly I'm even mad at Grandmother Oak.

"Mamma says you have to do the chores *right now.*" Daniel is squinting up into the tree, holding the wire pail for gathering eggs. He pushes his glasses up. His glasses are forever sliding down his nose.

I climb down, grumbling to myself. "What good is a thinking place if I never have time to use it?" I glare at Daniel. I can't be nice to him every single minute. Especially when nobody is nice to me. Well, *almost* nobody.

I grab the wire pail and stomp off to gather the eggs. I'm thinking so hard about school stuff that I forget to watch where I step. Oh *yuck!* I step into a blob of ishy-squishy chicken poop. Suddenly I'm furious with the hens. *"You're nothing but a bunch of chickens — yellow-bellied chickens!"* My yelling makes them flappity-squawk all over the place. I plunk right down on a bale of hay by the wall and kind of sniffle-sob. *"If there are birds in heaven,"* I shout, *"I hope none of them are chickens!*" They start their flappity-squawks all over again. I sit there a couple of minutes sniffling, then get back to work. The truth is, I don't really like chickens much. They are always gabble-babbling like a bunch of gossiping old ladies.

After gathering eggs, I help Papa milk. One of the cows, Dancer, follows Papa into the barn. Dancer loves Papa, and likes to follow him around. I grab a milk pail and sit down to milk Maggie. I like milking her best because her zum-zums are easy to hold onto, and her milk flows easily. Daniel and I call cows' teats zum-zums, because of the sound of milk streaming into the pail. *Zum-zum, zum-zum.* Our cat, Stinker, stands on her hind legs near Maggie's behind, waiting for me to squirt a stream of milk to her. She can stand that way forever. I aim a squirt at her. She laps it up. Milk drips from her chin. She looks so funny, I giggle. "At least *you're* my friend," I say.

"Something bothering you, my Rose?" Papa asks. Oops, didn't realize I had talked loud enough for Papa to hear. Wonder if I should ask him about war ... or what he did instead of going to war. I usually don't talk to Papa, and for sure not to Mamma, about stuff that's bothering me. Mostly I talk to Aunt Bette or Grandmother Oak. I hunch down and concentrate fiercely on milking. *Zum-zum, zum-zum*.

"Rose?" I almost can't hear Papa's voice above his *zum-zumming* and mine.

"Um ... Papa ... why don't you believe in going to war?"

"Well, my Rose, that's a big question." *Zum-zum, zum-zum*. "I don't believe in violence because it makes more violence. Even with the farm critters. Remember how Dancer used to kick every time I tried to milk her?"

"Uh-huh, she used to dance and prance about, and kick up such a fuss, that sometimes her foot landed right in the milk pail."

"That's right, Rose. I could have made a choice to beat her, or kick her right back." I can't help laughing at the picture in my head of Papa kicking a cow. "I got so mad at her sometimes that I was tempted to do just that. Once she kicked my leg so hard, I had a black-and-blue bruise for weeks." *Zum-zum, zum-zum.* Is it my imagination, or did his *zum-zums* just get louder?

"Papa, I never knew you felt like kicking Dancer. You always talked to her real quiet, and stroked her ... and never *ever* yelled."

"Well, it's all about patience. At first she sure didn't allow me to stroke her. She hated being milked because she didn't want to be touched. She used to belong to young Jeb Jacobs and I've seen how he treats his animals. He beats them. No wonder Dancer didn't want a living soul near her. Well, Dancer learned to trust me, and now she's the gentlest cow we own. I'm very fond of this old girl." Papa *zum-zums* a soft swish-swish into the frothing milk.

"But, Papa, maybe it's different with people."

"Well, I reckon not. I know for a fact that Jeb had a hard time with his dad. His dad drank — he liked his bottle of whiskey. When he was drunk, he was tough on his kids, even beat them sometimes. So I imagine Jeb has a lot of rage, and poor Dancer got the brunt of some of it."

"And maybe Jeb's papa was mean because *his* papa was mean to him."

"It's possible. That's exactly what I mean about violence making more violence."

Papa explaining about Dancer makes me think about Zippy. That's what I call the wild-eyed cat, because he zips away every time he sees me. "Papa," I say, "there is a wild, stray cat that comes around sometimes. Maybe somebody was mean to him. Maybe he'll learn to trust me ... like Dancer trusts you."

"I've seen that skittery kitty, too," says Papa. "Likely you'll be able to tame him. Can never be sure, though, with folks, or with critters, whether they'll warm up to you or not."

Stinker perches on her hind legs again. I laugh and aim another squirt. "I didn't have to tame you, Stinker. You trusted me ever since you were a teeny-tiny kitten."

"That's because she never learned to be afraid," says Papa. He gets up from milking the last cow.

All at once, I want to keep talking with Papa.

Quick, before he leaves, I blurt, "Papa, what kind of service do Mennonites do instead of going to war?"

He hangs the milk pail on a hook on the barn wall. Stinker rubs around and around his legs. Papa reaches down to pet her, then straightens up and looks at me. "Many conscientious objectors — those who have a conscience against war — work for CPS," he says. "That stands for Civilian Public Service. And, by the way, Mennonites are not the only ones who have a conscience against war. There are other groups and individuals who believe war makes things worse instead of solving things. But about CPS — there are lots of different work assignments. For example, some work in mental hospitals, some work in camps for soil conservation, some work in forestry. Those in forestry projects even fight forest fires."

"Forest fires? You'd have to be very brave to do that."

"Yes, it's dangerous. Conscientious objectors *must* face danger, and even death if necessary, just as soldiers do."

Papa continues, "Some join the military to work as ambulance drivers or medics to help the wounded. This is a way to give care and show compassion, but not carry guns. Some medics and ambulance drivers have been killed while serving in this way. But some conscientious objectors feel that being part of the military in any way supports the idea of war."

"But what did *you* do?"

"Well, I'll tell you about it. But it'll have to wait. I have to fix the tractor before supper."

"Did you fight forest —" He is already outside. In my head I see him fighting a huge fire that is even fiercer, and more dangerous, than Hitler.

Before going into the house, I take a bowl of milk behind the barn for Zippy. I sit up against the barn wall. Sure enough, after a while he peers at me from under a bush. I call in a soft voice, "You can come out. I won't hurt you." But he stays under the bush. That's okay. It's all about patience. Some day maybe he'll be brave enough to come right up to me. I sit as long as I dare.

Mamma is probably mad already that I haven't come to help with supper.

"Where have you *been?*" she asks when I finally come into the house.

"Doing my chores."

"Honestly, you're as slow as molasses in winter."

5

Big, Fat Blasphemy

"*Blessed are the peacemakers for they shall be called ...*"

... *yellow-bellied chickens*, I finish in my head.

"... *children of God,*" the preacher says.

But my own thoughts keep buzzing about in my head. *Stupid are the peacemakers for they shall be called yellow ... and coward ... and all stuff like that!* I sigh. I probably did a big, fat blasphemy by thinking that. But I didn't mean to think anything against God. It's just that things are so hard at school. Wonder if I could get thrown out of church, or kicked out, for thinking that blasphemy. Papa told me how some folks got kicked out of church for not believing the same stuff as other Mennonites. That means that they were not allowed to come to church anymore, not that they were actually thrown out the window, or kicked out the door. But in my imagination, I see a great big guy who opens the church door, puts the person in front of it, takes a running start like a football player, and boots her right out the door. And — *zoom* — the person goes flying.

"Blessed are ye when men revile you and persecute you ..."

I got persecuted in school, but I don't *feel* blessed. I just feel smad. That's a word I made up last year. It means sad and mad all mixed together. I think I'd rather have friends than be blessed.

" ... and say all kinds of evil against you falsely for my sake. Rejoice and be glad ..."

What? I'm supposed to be glad? That doesn't even make sense!

"... for great is your reward in heaven. This Scripture reading is from Matthew five."

But heaven is so long to wait. Another sigh. Oops, too loud. Mamma sends me a blazing look. Daniel is sitting between her and me. Papa sits next to me on the other side.

Uh-oh! A tiny snore from Papa. Papa nods off to sleep in church sometimes. It makes Mamma boiling mad. Maybe I should wake him up before he does a big rumbling snore. Oh, well, let him sleep. Maybe he needs sleep more than he needs a sermon. He already knows how to be peaceful. He'll probably get heaps of rewards in heaven.

After the Bible reading, there is lots of standing up and sitting down, depending on whether we're praying, singing, or what. Papa calls all the standing up and sitting down, "church calisthenics." "Calisthenics" means doing exercises to stay in shape. I smile to myself at Papa's joke.

We stand for a song. "*When peace like a river, attendeth my way ...*"

We sit for taking the offering.

We stand for a prayer.

Up and down. Up and down.

When we stand for the prayer, I happen to glance at Mamma. What's the matter with her? Her face is red and her eyes blaze at me again. Could she have somehow figured out the blasphemy I was thinking a little while ago? She's pointing at Papa, but her hands are down low, as if she doesn't want anyone else to see. Uh-oh! Papa is still sitting — and sleeping. I poke him gently.

"Oh!" Papa says, right out loud. He looks around, confused. Then gets up. A kid behind us snickers. Mamma's face gets redder. Papa's going to get it from Mamma when we get home. He sure messed up with his church calisthenics this time.

Finally the sermon starts. This is when things usually get really boring. I count bald heads and look at the women's hats down below. We're sitting in the balcony. Most of the hats are boring — black, navy blue, or brown. Except for Aunt Bette's. There it is, a big, bright orange hat. People call her Big Hat Bette. Most folks in our church think wearing bright, flashy stuff is the sin of pride. Aunt Bette does lots of other stuff that folks from our church don't do, like going to the theatre. Oh, and she has paintings of naked people in her house. Lots of the people around here don't approve of Aunt Bette's ways. But I do.

The sermon drones on. I decide to play the

what-would-happen-if game in my head. What would happen if I walked along the balcony railing as if it were a tightrope? Hurry, hurry, hurry folks. Step right up and see Rose, the amazing, death-defying acrobat. This has been my best what-would-happen-if, ever since Aunt Bette took me to a circus last summer. Mamma thought the circus was the biggest *Dummheit* ever. *Dummheit* is a German word that means silliness. What would happen if I juggled my Sunday School coins, maybe while walking along the railing? Would I drop the coins? Or maybe I'd come crashing down right on top of peoples' heads. Would I get kicked out of church for causing such a big commotion?

Before I can think of any more what-would-happen-ifs, I actually get interested in the sermon. The preacher is talking about recruitment. "It is especially disturbing that there is army recruitment even now when the U.S. is not at war. If we treat the world as a field of battle, surely we are inviting, even creating, the very thing we fear. Let us not invite war by taking up arms, but invite peace by taking a stand for justice." Hmmm ... the words spin around in my head.

Then the preacher says other stuff about how Jesus told us to love our enemies and do good to those who hurt us. And he says that in the Ten Commandments — actually our church has a gazillion commandments — it says "thou shalt not kill," and it doesn't say "thou shalt not kill unless you feel unsafe, or are afraid of being killed yourself." I think about this. I guess it would be brave, all right, not to kill someone, even though they might kill you. He ends with, "As it says in the Scriptures, *blessed are the peacemakers* ..." Uh-oh! I agreed with some of the stuff he said. But did he have to add that last part? What would happen if I got right up and shouted, "Stupid are the peacemakers, for they shall be called yellow-bellied chickens?" That big blasphemy again. I almost feel like crying. I'm so befuddled in my mind about war and stuff.

Daniel and I sit in the back seat of the car on the way home from church. Daniel sings, "*God sees the witto sparrow faw*." Then he adds, "I know why God didn't pick up that witto sparrow that got dead."

"And why's that?" asks Papa.

"Because He's got no hands." We laugh. Daniel makes a pouty face. I guess we hurt his feelings. "My Sunday Skoo teacher said God isn't wike a person, with hands and feet and ... and stuff."

"Well, my boy," says Papa, "if God isn't exactly like a person, that means that we have to be God's hands and feet, and we have to do the things that need to be done in this old world."

"But ... but ..." Daniel's eyes are moving back and forth like mad. He looks really worried. "... If God isn't wike a person, maybe He's got no eyes. So how can He see the witto sparrow faw?" We laugh again. "Stop waffing at me."

I put my arm around him. "Maybe God is so great, that He doesn't even need eyes to see," I say.

"Oh." He curls into me, and smiles. His eyes get twinkly. "Does God got toes?"

"Don't be ridiculous," says Mamma. Her voice

is sharp. I pull Daniel closer to me.

He whispers into my ear, "Does God got a bewy button?"

"I don't know if He has a belly button," I whisper back. Daniel's jingly giggle fills the car.

*　*　*

I'm behind the barn with a bowl of milk, waiting for Zippy. I put the bowl halfway between me and the bush where he sometimes hides. I have the whole afternoon. I love Sunday afternoons because no one is bothering me to do work. "On the seventh day the Lord rested," says our preacher, "and so must we." I'm not going to argue with that.

While I wait, I read *Little House on the Prairie*. I like Laura, the kid in the book. She's spunky, almost like Anne, in *Anne of Green Gables*.

I haven't seen Zippy yet, but I call out softly every once in awhile, in case he knows my voice — and knows there will be milk. And then — oh! — when I look up from reading, there he is. He's crouching under the bush, his eyes wide. He looks from me to the bowl of milk. I talk in a soft voice. "It's okay, Zippy. Don't be afraid." He creeps forward a tiny bit.

I barely breathe. I don't move a muscle. My nose itches. I don't dare scratch. Why did my nose have to start itching right now? Zippy creeps a little closer, his belly close to the ground. He doesn't take his eyes off me. The itch gets worse. I ignore my nose, but my nose doesn't ignore me. It's driving me crazy. Zippy inches forward. He's almost there. I keep talking softly. Maybe if he gets all the way to the milk, he won't notice if I scratch my nose. He's there. And — oh, oh, oh! — he's lapping it up. Slowly, slowly I lift my hand and scratch. Me and my nose are so happy!

6

Speechify and Preachify

"Aunt Bette, I might have done a blasphemy." I'm visiting at her house.

She raises one eyebrow, and has an almost-smile. "Oh?"

"Do people get kicked out of church, or thrown out of church, for blasphemy?"

"Sometimes, but if you get thrown out of church, I'll talk to the person in charge of throwing. I'll make sure you don't get thrown from the balcony window. It's just a short drop from the first-floor window." She's grinning.

"Aunt Bette! I'm serious!"

"I'm sorry darlin'. Come here." She pats the place next to her on her flowered couch. I sit, and she pulls me towards her and puts her arms around me. "Now what's this all about?"

"Um ... you know when the preacher read the part in the Bible about *blessed are the peacemakers for they shall be called children of God?* Well, I thought *stupid* are the peacemakers for they shall be called yellow-bellied chickens."

She laughs. *Laughs!*

"Aunt *Bette*," I wail.

She turns to me and holds my face between her two hands. Her eyes are soft. I wish Mamma looked at me that way sometimes. "You can be sure I've had thoughts like that, too."

"You have?"

"Of course, sweetheart." She hugs me a little closer. "God can handle your anger. And, no, you won't get thrown out of church. I know your heart is in the right place." She is quiet for a while, then asks, "Has someone called you names, or been unkind to you?"

I stare at a big, purple flower on the couch. Finally I blurt, "The kids call me 'yellow' and 'chicken' and nasty stuff like that." And before I know it, I'm telling her lots of stuff — how Mr. Foster yelled at me for joking that Uncle Sam didn't look like my uncle, how the kids don't understand about Mennonites not believing in war, how even Cindy doesn't like me anymore, and how kids call Papa a coward because he wasn't in the war. I even admit to her that I called Judy's papa a killer.

Suddenly I'm almost shouting. "And you know what, Aunt Bette? Sometimes I think the kids and Mr. Foster are right. It's just *stupid* not to go to war. How can we stay safe and ... um ... sanctimonious ..." A tiny smile flashes across Aunt Bette's face, then disappears. "... when others go to war for us. Maybe Hitler would have taken over the *whole world* if other folks hadn't gone to war."

"Safe and sanctimonious?" Now she looks sad. "May God forgive us when — if — this is true. When the situation calls for it, we must *absolutely* be as brave as any soldier. And that includes a willingness to die." She is quiet for a long time.

Finally she says, "It's right for you to question

your views on war. There are more questions than answers in this old world. At some point you'll form your own belief. This is my belief. I'm against violence of any kind — day to day. When your teacher humiliates and embarrasses you in front of the class, that's violence. When Judy taunts you, that's violence. And darlin'," she says gently, "when you call Judy's papa a killer, that's violence."

I look down, ashamed. "I know," I say in a small voice. "But, Aunt Bette, what about whole, big wars, between *countries* — not just stuff that happens in school?"

"Darlin', I believe there is a *strong* connection between what we do every day and the bigger question of war. When even parents and teachers yell and beat their kids, children naturally think that fighting — being tougher and bigger — is the way to solve problems. If that's what they learn in their homes and schools, of course they'll think that is the way to solve problems between countries. We may not be able to stop a war, but we can choose how to act in school and at home.

And we can choose whether or not to participate in war. We are fortunate to have other ways to serve our country.

"Goodness, Rose, you've got me speechifying and preachifying." She smiles at me. "Sometimes I wish our preacher would break up his preachifying with a little ... lightness — even fun and frolic. Sometimes I need to wiggle the kinks out of my old bones, or I can't listen anymore." She gets up, and does a jiggly little dance. Her bracelets jingle and her earrings jangle.

"You look funny," I say.

"Good! Want to join me? We'll look funny together."

I get up and do a wiggle-jig with her. "What would happen if we danced down the aisles at church when the sermon gets boring?" I ask. Aunt Bette laughs. Soon we sit down again.

Aunt Bette gets a thinking look. Furrows run across her forehead. "We *must* be willing to ..."

"Sounds like you're going to speechify and preachify again, Aunt Bette."

"You're absolutely right. I'm doing it again."

"That's okay, Aunt Bette. You preachify much better than our preacher preachifies."

She bursts out laughing. "That's the best compliment I've had in a long time."

"Besides," I add, "when the preacher preachifies, he doesn't have jingle-jangle jewellery that I can watch."

"Well, as I was preachifying ..." She waggles her head to make her earrings jingle. "Can't leave out that touch, since the preacher isn't able to provide it."

Suddenly Aunt Bette's face changes — gets all serious. She stops and stares into the distance. Then she looks straight into my eyes. She talks slowly. "We *must* be willing to die for what we believe, but we must *never* kill for what we believe. When we think we are killing for a good reason, we are only fooling ourselves."

Her words kind of settle inside me. I don't know how to explain the big feeling in my belly. I roll her words around in my head. *We must be willing to die for what we believe, but never kill for what we believe.* We are both quiet for a long time.

Finally she says, "Your eccentric, big-hatted Aunt Bette is a hopeless speechifyer. Guess we won't solve the world's problems this afternoon."

"I'm gonna be eccentric like you when I grow up."

She laughs. "You're well on your way, my dear. But you are eccentric like *you* — not like me."

Before Aunt Bette takes me home, we go to her garden. She has big flowers — mums, huge roses, and, in the summer, peonies. Come to think of it, everything about Aunt Bette is big — her hats, her skirts, her garden, her laugh. Her bosom is big, too, and soft to sink into. I smile thinking of this. She's a huggy person, not like Mamma and Papa, who aren't the hug-and-snuggle type.

We sit on a garden bench. The roses in front of us nod in the wind.

"I love this garden," says Aunt Bette. "It calms me when I'm upset."

"Oh, just like when I'm in the branches of Grandmother Oak."

"We all need a special thinking place."

I feel good in Aunt Bette's garden — in this piece of forever. "Each minute is a piece of forever." I say this out loud to Aunt Bette.

She smiles a big smile. "What a wonderful thought." The roses keep nodding their heads up and down, up and down, as if they agree.

"That makes every minute *important*," I say.

"Sure does."

Yes, yes, yes, nod the roses.

* * *

Back home, while gathering the eggs, Aunt Bette's words churn in my head. "You know what, you chickens?" I say. "We must be willing to *die* for what we believe, but we must never *kill* for what we believe."

I'm feeling so good after coming home from Aunt Bette's place, that I even feel friendly towards these old hens. I decide to apologize for shouting a few days ago. "I'm sorry I yelled at you the other day. You do lots of flutter-flapping and gabble-babbling, but you can't help it that you were born chickens. I guess God made you to be chickens, and me to be a girl. And I've never even *seen* a chicken with a yellow belly in my whole life." One old, speckled hen tilts her head and looks up at me with one side of her face. She clucks in a scolding way. I guess she was really insulted that I'd called her 'yellow-bellied.' "Well, I *said* I'm sorry." She murmurs, quieter now. I think I'm forgiven.

After gathering eggs, there's milking. Chores never end. Papa and I both *zum-zum* into our pails. Maybe this is a good time to talk about what he did instead of fighting in the war. "Papa, when you were in CPS camp, did you fight raging forest fires?"

"No, 'fraid not, my Rose."

"Oh." *Zum-zum, zum-zum.* I hear the sag in my voice, then feel ashamed. But I had imagined him driving huge fire trucks — he is really good at driving big trucks — and fighting fearlessly in roaring, crackling fires. "Fighting fires must have been awfully dangerous." Why don't I be quiet already?

"Uh-huh, from what some of the fellows say, the men parachuted very near the fiery areas."

I gasp.

"Rose, the CPS camp where I worked was a soil conservation project. I was recruited into the project by the CPS board, who'd heard that I had a knack for that sort of thing." Papa sounds proud, but not in a nasty way. He smiles, and even blushes a little. "We found ways to keep our good earth from being blown or washed away — figured out what trees and grasses to plant to hold the soil. Also found ways of preserving the nutrients in the earth to build up the soil. The whole idea of the various CPS projects was to build things up, rather than tear things down."

"Is that all you did?" Why don't I stop blathering? I don't want to hurt his feelings.

"Well I scrubbed lots and lots of pots and pans in the CPS kitchen."

Scrubbed pots and pans? This is getting worse. I'll never tell the kids *that*.

"I'm afraid that's one thing that stands out in my memory. Stacks and piles of pots and pans."

"Papa, did folks ever make fun of you? Call you 'chicken' and stuff?"

"Yes, Rose." He looks real sad. "Some of the guys made life real miserable for me."

"What did they do, Papa?"

"Oh, they beat up on me some." Then he adds, "The work of peacemaking isn't always ... peaceful."

He turns his face away and leaves the barn in a hurry.

I sigh. Maybe I shouldn't have reminded him about that hard time in his life. I shouldn't have kept ranting on about fire-fighting. I probably just made him feel bad.

7

Run Out of the Country

The next morning in school, as Sandra and I walk into the schoolyard, Cindy ignores us. She hasn't been exactly nasty to me lately — just pretends I don't exist. She goes to a group of kids who are sitting on the school steps. "My brother left for training in Fort Riley," she says.

"Guess you'll miss him," says Tom.

"Your brother's gonna make sure our country stays safe," says Judy. Seeing me, she yells, "Not like some folks who went to some stupid camp! Hey, Rose, what did your papa do at that camp besides making macaroni necklaces?"

Sandra stops walking. "Come on," I say, pretending I'm not scared. We walk up to the group. I sit on the steps. Sandra stays standing. Ignoring my hammering heart, I say, "My papa worked in soil conservation. He figured out stuff like what grasses to plant so soil wouldn't wash away and —"

"*Soil conservation?*" sneers Judy. "*My* papa was fighting in the front lines, while *your* papa ..." She grins a nasty grin. "... was playing around in the dirt."

Some of the kids laugh.

"Playing around in the dirt," repeats Judy. "Maybe he made some mud pies along with the macaroni necklaces at that stupid camp."

Some kids start to holler out stuff.

"He sure didn't have to risk his life like *my* papa."

"Your papa is a coward."

I hate this, hate this, hate this! Why couldn't Papa have fought forest fires or driven an ambulance or something? I can't think what to say, and Sandra is sure no help. She is just staring at the ground. And Cindy! She isn't yelling nasty stuff, but she isn't sticking up for me either. Last year she would have.

The bell rings, and all the kids hurry off to class. I catch up to Cindy. "Some friend you turned out to be," I say.

She looks down. "My papa thinks ..."

"Your papa, your papa, your papa!" I'm shouting. *"I'm tired of hearing about your papa ... and everyone else's papa, and how much better you think they are than mine. My papa loves our country and so do I!"*

"Well, what am I supposed to think? He's my papa." Now *she* is shouting. She kicks a pebble — sends it flying. "He says to stay away from the likes of you." Then her voice gets real quiet, and mean. "He says folks like you should be run out of the country."

Run out of the country? I'm too stunned to say anything at all. My head feels all buzzy. I turn away and shuffle into the schoolroom. I hang my head. I don't feel spunky anymore.

Uncle Sam glares at me from the poster hanging up front. His bony finger points right at me. He makes me feel guilty — just like Mr. Foster and the kids do. He's probably thinking, *people like you should be run out of the country.*

We're supposed to be choosing a current events project. I take my *Current Events Newsletter* from my desk. The words blur together. I put the newsletter back into my desk. I decide to push Cindy's words right out of my head, so I can get through the day.

Later in this horrible day, Mr. Foster says, "I have something important to tell you." Nothing feels important to me, right now. "We are going to express our gratitude to our veterans, those who have served in recent wars, by having a Veterans Day assembly here at Prairie View Elementary. We will have it on Friday, November 9, because Veterans Day is on a Sunday. Reverend Jewett, the Methodist minister, will speak to us, and some of you will be asked to be on the program — perhaps recite a poem or sing. Each of you will write a letter to a local veteran to invite him or her to this event."

Write a letter? A veteran would hate me for sure, like Cindy's papa does. Sandra looks at me. Her eyes are big and scared-looking. I look away. I can't think about this right now. *People like you*

63

should be run out of the country. Trying to push those words away isn't working.

"Of course," Mr. Foster continues, "some of your fathers and brothers will get special invitations. If you have a veteran you wish to invite, either a family member or friend, be sure to tell me. If you don't know who to invite, talk to me and I will give you a name."

What am I supposed to do? Is it against my beliefs to write this kind of letter? What would Mamma and Papa say about it? Or our preacher? What do *I* say about it? I look at Sandra again. She is staring down at her desk, like she always does when she's embarrassed, or feels bad about something. And all the while, Cindy's words keep popping into my head. I can't help it. *Run out of the country.*

As we walk home from school, I don't tell Sandra about what Cindy said. I just can't make myself talk about it.

Sandra says, "You're not going to write a letter to a veteran, are you?"

"I don't know."

"Well, you better not, because war is against our religion."

"Writing a letter is *not* against my religion." I glare at her. "Yes, I'm going to write a letter." I just decided this minute, because it makes me mad that Sandra is so sure about this. And about other stuff. Anyway, I don't think this is a yes-or-no question. I think it's a maybe question.

After chores, I sit behind the barn again, with a bowl of milk. I do this every chance I get, putting the bowl a bit closer to me each time. Finally Zippy comes, drinks the milk quickly, then hurries to sit under a bush. I wish it wouldn't take him so long to trust me. I talk to him in a calm voice. "Was somebody mean to you? Did someone call you nasty names? Or throw something at you? Maybe chase you away with a pitchfork?" Zippy perks his ears towards me. "Did some mean old guy yell 'cats like you ought to be run out of the country?'" I make my voice as soothing as I can. "Well *I* think cats like you ought to be treated *real* gently."

8

Discovering Sadako

Cindy is back to pretending I don't exist. Uncle Sam still glares, Judy is still nasty, and Sandra and I still don't know what to do for our current events project. Nothing in school is fun now that lots of kids don't like me anymore. Every time I see Cindy, I think of those horrible words she said to me.

I might as well think about the current events project. I'll have to talk to Sandra and see if she has any ideas. I look at the headlines in the *Current Events Newsletter.*

`Interstate Highway System Underway`
Boring!

`Evangelist Billy Graham in`
`Oklahoma City`

Already too much preachifying in my life.

Ed Sullivan Show Hosts Elvis

Hmmm. Now that would be fun! Sandra and I could surprise everyone with a little wiggle-jiggle rock 'n' roll for our 'artistic component.' *Don't Be Cruel*. I heard Elvis Presley sing that on the radio Papa bought. He bought it even though Mamma said having a radio was much too worldly. We don't have a television though. We could never, ever convince Mamma to get one. Anyway, Sandra would never agree to an Elvis project.

I'm about to give up, when, on the very last page, I see something.

Statue Erected for 12-year-old in Hiroshima

Sadako Sasaki was only twelve years old when she died of the atom-bomb disease.

She was only a bit older than I am.

Born in 1943, she was two years old when the atom bomb destroyed Hiroshima. Sadako didn't seem hurt

at the time, but ten years later
she developed leukemia — sometimes
called the atom-bomb disease — as a
result of radiation from the bomb.
She died in 1955.

That was just last year! Something churns in my belly. I feel — I don't know — connected to her or something. Being almost the same age and everything. I'll soon be eleven.

Plans for a statue of Sadako are
underway. It will be erected in
Hiroshima's Peace Park. The statue
is in remembrance of Sadako and all
the children who died as a result
of the bomb. New cases of the radiation sickness are appearing even
now.

I have a big hunk of sadness in my belly.

Sadako was an active girl, well
liked by all, and was especially
skilled in sports. She was a
runner.

She sounds so spunky.

Japanese legend says that if a sick person folds 1,000 paper cranes, they will be healed. Sadako began folding cranes, but became too sick to reach her goal of 1,000. She died on October 25, 1955.

I think about Sadako folding cranes so she'd get well, but dying anyway. *It's* not *fair.* I have a sobby feeling in my throat. Why was Sadako born where a bomb was dropped, and I was born here, in a safe place? So many things I don't know. But I know one thing. Sadako's story will be my current events project, if I can get Sandra to agree. But how can we find out more about Sadako and the bomb? I wonder if I can convince Mamma or Papa to take me to the McPherson city library. Probably not. But it doesn't hurt to try.

All at once I realize that when I was reading about Sadako, I didn't once think about the horrible thing Cindy said.

After school, I talk to Sandra about Sadako. She agrees right away that it is a good project.

* * *

"I need to go to the McPherson library to do research for a current events project." Mamma and I are washing dishes after supper.

"*Ach*, no! We're far too busy to go traipsing to McPherson."

"But, Mamma, this is *important*." I try to think of something that will convince her. "The project will show how war causes bad things."

"Oh?" She looks up. Maybe she'll actually consider it. *I hope! I hope! I hope!*

"Sandra and I are doing a project about this girl named Sadako from Japan who died because of the war, even though she didn't do anything wrong." I tell her everything I read in the *Current Events Newsletter*.

Mamma sighs. "I don't see how we can take time right now for a trip to the library."

A trip to town is a big deal at our house. We have to plan it forever, as if we were going around the whole world or something.

"We need to gather the fall crops — dig out the carrots, potatoes, and turnips. Your papa still has field work before winter ..." She keeps listing more and more farm stuff that has to be done.

"Maybe Aunt Bette can take me. Oh, and Sandra, too." Why didn't I think of this before? With Aunt Bette, we'd probably do other stuff besides going to the library — maybe even eat at a restaurant. With Mamma and Papa, we sure wouldn't. We'd go straight to the library, and Mamma would be hurry-upping me the whole time. Then we'd rush home to milk the cows, gather eggs, feed the pigs, and do a thousand other farm chores. I am worried though, that even if Aunt Bette agrees, Sandra's mamma and papa might not let her come.

Mamma's forehead wrinkles. She's *thinking* about it!

"Oh *please, please, please!* I'll ask Aunt Bette."

"I'm sure you will. Well, give her a call. But finish the dishes first."

"Whoop-de-do and hallelujah!" I'm almost sure Aunt Bette will take us. She goes to town all the time. She even goes to movies sometimes. What if she took us to a *movie?* The thought of that boggles my mind. I've never been to a movie in my whole life. Well, Mamma would never allow that. Papa might — if it were something like *The Ten Commandments*.

9

Dummheit Is *Dummheit*

"*You ain't nothin' but a hound dog.*" We're in the kitchen when an Elvis Presley song comes on the radio. I wiggle my hips and waggle my whole body. I'm so crazy happy about going to McPherson with Aunt Bette. It's for sure now. *Who needs Cindy? I can be happy without her.* Aunt Bette is taking Sandra and me in a couple of days. I'm surprised that Sandra's mamma is letting her go.

"I'm a hound dog," sings Daniel. He wiggles and waggles too. "Woof! Woof!"

"I knew we shouldn't have gotten a radio," says Mamma. "It just teaches our children lots of *Dummheit.*"

"Mamma, do you ever do *Dummheit?*" I ask.

"You'll never catch *her* doing anything silly," says Papa. His eyes tease.

"I could 'do *Dummheit*,' as you say, as well as the rest of you if it weren't so ..."

"... so *Dummheit?*" Papa winks at me. "Mamma thinks *Dummheit* is *Dummheit.*"

I laugh.

Mamma glares at Papa. She stands up and is quiet for a minute, looking into the distance. I think that maybe she's looking into the past. Then she steps forward, as if walking onto a stage or something, and belts out, *"Mairzy doats and dosy doats ..."* I can't believe it! Daniel's eyes bug out. Papa has a huge grin.

Daniel giggles. "What's a dosydoats?"

Mamma ignores him. "*... and little lambsydivey ...*" All at once Mamma's voice gets quieter.

"What's a wamsydivey?"

Mamma still doesn't answer him. "*A kiddleydivey too ...*" Mamma's voice gets wobbly and she stops singing. What's happening to her face? Her lips are trembling. Papa goes to her and puts his hands on her shoulders. *Hug her, hug her,*

74

hug her, I say inside my head. But he just stands with his hands on her shoulders. She turns and goes into the bedroom. Papa follows.

"What's the matter with Mamma?" asks Daniel.

"Maybe she's sad about stuff from long ago." Aunt Bette once told me that Mamma's papa wouldn't allow her to do readings and poems and stuff at school programs, even though she was real good at it. I was so surprised when Aunt Bette told me that.

"What stuff from wong ago?"

"Mamma's papa didn't allow her to do lots of fun stuff like poems and silly songs. He got real mad if she did stuff like that. She even got punished." Daniel's eyes are moving back and forth like mad as he puzzles about this.

When Mamma comes out of the bedroom, Daniel runs to her and hugs her around her legs — that's as far up as he can reach. "I wike the funny song you sang," he says in a quieter-than-usual voice.

She touches the top of his head, but doesn't

say anything. Daniel doesn't ask her to sing the *Mairzy doats* song again. I think he doesn't want to upset her.

"I like it too, Mamma," I say quietly. I don't want to upset her either. She smiles at me.

*   *   *

After supper Mamma seems back to her usual self — busy and bustling about the kitchen. "Mamma, will you sing that funny song again?" asks Daniel.

"Not now, you little *Schnickelfritz.*"

But Papa looks up from *The Farm Journal* and drones "*Mairzy doats and dosy doats ...*" It sounds awful. Papa's voice is all on one note.

Mamma throws up her hands. "Heaven help us!" She looks at Daniel and me. "Your papa thinks I can't be silly." She looks at Papa. "*I'll* show you some *Dummheit!*" She sings again. "*Mairzy doats and dosy doats ...*" She takes her apron off and waves it back and forth in front of her. Can this be happening? "*... and little lambsy-divey ...*" Mamma sways. She's almost dancing. "*A kiddleydivey too, wouldn't you? A kiddleydivey too, wouldn't you?*" Daniel and I are both laughing our

76

heads off. Papa is grinning. Mamma sings real good. But Papa ... oh my!

"You're better than Elvis Presley," I say. "Again! Again!" says Daniel.

We all join Mamma. I grab a kettle and spoon, and beat the rhythm.

"Me too! I wanna do that!" shouts Daniel. I give him the kettle and spoon. Daniel bangs. Papa drones. I wiggle-waggle. Papa does a jerky little wiggle. It's the funniest time *ever*. So why am I almost crying?

"What's a mairzydoats?" asks Daniel.

"*Ach, das ist ganz verrückt*," says Mamma. That means "completely crazy." But she is smiling.

Daniel puts his hands on his hips like Mamma does sometimes. "But what's a *mairzydoats? Nobody wissens* to me." We all laugh and Daniel makes a pouty mouth.

Papa comes to his rescue. "What does it sound like when you say 'mares eat oats' real fast?"

"Mairzydoats." Daniel's face lights up. "O-o-oh!"

"And see what happens when you say the rest

of these words real fast." Papa goes through the whole song until Daniel figures out what the words mean.

"Mares eat oats ... and does eat oats ... And little lambs eat ivy ... A kid will eat ivy, too. Wouldn't you?"

10

Befuddled In My Mind

Mr. Foster gave me the name and address of a Mr. Lambert to invite to the Veterans Day assembly, even though I don't know him. I didn't tell Mamma and Papa about having to write a letter, or about the Veterans Day assembly. But I told Aunt Bette. I told her I couldn't figure out what to write. She said to speak from my heart. Sandra doesn't have to write a letter because her mamma wrote a note that she wasn't allowed.

Dear Mr. Lambert,

Thank you for being in the war.

I cross that out. I don't know whether to say thank you, or what, since my family doesn't believe in war. I start again. This is about the thousandth time I've started over. My pencil has lots of teeth marks. I've been biting it like I used to when I was a little kid.

We are going to have a Veterans Day assembly at our school, Prairie View Elementary, on Friday, November 9, at 1:00 p.m. I hope you can come.

Now what should I say?

I think you were very brave for being in the war.

Yeah, I can leave that part. It's true, for sure. Now what? Speak from my heart.

But I have to admit that I'm all befuddled in my mind about war. I'm trying to figure out what I believe about it. My family is Mennonite and Mennonites don't believe in going to war.

I wonder what Mr. Lambert thinks about Mennonites. What if he thinks we should be run out of the country?

But I'm confused, because Hitler was doing terrible things and sure had to be stopped. But some things about war are just too awful. Like the bomb on Hiroshima. Do you know about Sadako? She was a girl from Hiroshima. She died last year from the atom-bomb disease, even though

she didn't do anything wrong. I keep thinking
about her because she was almost the same age as
I am. Anyway, my papa and some of his friends
did other things to serve our country because we
are conscientious objectors. Papa worked in a CPS
camp and found ways to help the soil from wash-
ing away.

I don't mention that he scrubbed pots and pans.

I hope you don't think he is a yellow-bellied
chicken. Sometimes the other kids call me a
yellow-bellied chicken.

I cross out the last sentence so hard I make a hole
in the paper. I glare down at my paper.

"Are you having trouble with your letter,
Rose?" asks Mr. Foster. His voice is almost kind.

"Yes, sir," I say in a choky voice. He looks kind
of sorry, but doesn't say anything. He just nods.
Suddenly I think that maybe it's because he
doesn't know what to say — I mean because of my
beliefs and all. Maybe he's not such a bad teacher,
though I still wish we had our last year's teacher,
Mr. Ford, instead.

I go back to my letter. I decide to put back the

sentence I just crossed out because I'm just speaking from my heart.

Sometimes the kids call me a yellow-bellied chicken.

Uh-oh, I'm chewing my pencil again.

Anyway, I'm so sorry about all the soldiers that were killed, and about Hitler killing all those people. Did you have buddies who died in the war? I feel sad just thinking about the war. I even feel smad. That's a word I made up last year. It means being sad and mad at the same time. I will see you at the assembly. I'll be there because I'm smad, even though nobody died at my house, except sometimes our cats or other animals. But that doesn't count next to something as big as a war. Oh, the other day I helped my little brother with a funeral when a bird died, but that probably doesn't count either.

Sincerely, Rose

P.S. Some of the Mennonites in the CPS camps fought forest fires, and that was also very brave. They had to parachute right into the smoky, fiery parts.

After school, Cindy comes towards me, like maybe she wants to talk to me. I get all nervous. But then, she stops and goes the other way. I decide I'm glad she stopped, in case she was going to say something nasty. But I wonder ... does she want to make up?

That evening, Aunt Bette comes over after we've just finished supper. "Hi there, darlin'." She gives me a big hug. "Your mamma around?"

"Yeah, in the kitchen." I follow Aunt Bette into the house.

"Hannah," — that's Mamma's name — "about tomorrow's library trip — thought I'd take the girls to the Wichita library instead of the one in McPherson. It's bigger with a better selection."

"*Ach*, no. That's too far ... and so much traffic. It's too hard to drive in *Wichita!*"

"Oh *please, please, please*, Mamma," I say. I've never been to Wichita. About the only town I've ever been to in my whole life is McPherson. Wichita is a really big city in Kansas.

Papa is still at the table having coffee. Maybe he'll speak up for me.

"Oh, Hannah," says Aunt Bette. "I've often driven in Wichita. And Rose and Sandra are doing an important project — showing the terrible effects of war, in a way children can understand."

"But *Wichita?* I don't know. In Wichita there is so much ... temptation."

"Darlin'," says Aunt Bette to Mamma. Aunt Bette even calls grown-ups 'darlin'. "... they'll be with *me.*"

"That's what I'm afraid of," mutters Mamma.

"I'll lead them only into *acceptable* temptations." She grins.

"*Ach*, to you, *anything* is acceptable."

"Temptations, huh," says Papa. "Well I'm kinda tempted myself. If the fields weren't calling, I'd ride along. Go to that fancy library. Also see the new John Deere tractors at the Wichita outlet."

"Your old tractor is perfectly good."

"The point is, let her go." *Yippee!* "It will help our Rose and Sandra with their project."

All at once I'm bouncing up and down like a little kid. I can't help it. "Please!"

"But she'll get home so *late*."

"I've got that problem solved, too," says Aunt Bette. "The girls can stay at my house tomorrow night and then come to church with me on Sunday morning."

"But then she needs to pack." Mamma always makes a big deal about everything.

"She's not preparing for a year in Africa." I almost burst out laughing, but know that if I do, it might make Mamma madder, and she for sure wouldn't let me go to Wichita. "All she needs is a change of clothing and a toothbrush. Oh, and she can bring that *Current Events Newsletter* that tells about Sadako." Then Aunt Bette goes to Mamma, drapes her arms around her shoulders and says, "How can you refuse, when even Alma has agreed to let Sandra go?" Alma is Sandra's mamma.

"I can't imagine how you managed to convince her," says Mamma. Sandra's mamma is even stricter than mine.

"I have my ways."

Mamma throws up her hands. "Well, go then! You're all in cahoots." I smile to myself. I know

85

what the word means — a bunch of people agreeing, and sticking together about something. Mamma turns to wash the dishes. Pots and pans bang and clang. Maybe Mamma thinks we are all against her. I don't want her to think that. I quickly go to help her.

"Thank you, Mamma," I say in a small voice. "I wish you were happy about this like me."

"Oh, Rose." Her voice is almost soft. She wipes her hands on her apron and turns to me. She touches my hair. She started doing that last year — the closest she ever gets to hugging, though I do remember her hugging me just once. But right now she looks so sad. Maybe she really does think something awful will happen to me in Wichita. I give her a hug, and she gives me a quick little squeeze back. *The second time in my whole life!* Her hug is all stiff, but a hug is a hug. "I'm sure you'll do a good project," she says. Then she quickly turns away, like she's embarrassed or something.

In bed that night, I'm so excited about going to the library, that I can't get to sleep for ages.

Also, I'm worried about my letter to Mr. Lambert. Maybe it was really *dumb* to write that kind of letter to a veteran. He'll probably be real mad at me like lots of other folks around here. And I wish I hadn't used that stupid word, 'smad.' I thought it was such a good word when I made it up, but now it just seems dumb, and childish. Still, I guess writing a letter like that was brave.

And that reminds me. Zippy is getting braver. Today I put the milk closer than ever, and he did come. He didn't seem quite as nervous either.

11

Horror and Bedazzlement

Aunt Bette, Sandra, and I are at the Wichita Library. I've never seen so many books in one place in my whole life. I wonder if I could figure out the why of things if I read all these books. Probably not. Books don't know everything, and they don't always agree about stuff. I'll bet the books don't even agree about war, just like people around here don't agree about war.

There is oodles of stuff about the bomb and World War II. We find a whole magazine about the bomb on Hiroshima. I open the magazine and gasp. I slam it shut. Aunt Bette puts her hand on my shoulder. I open it again. I have to look, if I'm going to do the project. Sandra looks, too, and kind of moans. There are flattened buildings, and fire and dead people all over the place — even an arm with no body. But the saddest picture of all is of a little boy, about as big as Daniel, standing beside a dead woman — maybe his mamma. He is wearing nothing but a raggedy shirt. His arms and legs are bleeding and he is crying hard. There is smoke all around him.

"This is horrible," I whisper.

"I know, darlin'," says Aunt Bette in a soft voice.

I make myself look at more pictures. They are horrible, horrible, horrible! There is a huge, dark cloud. The words under it call it a "mushroom cloud," I guess because that's how it's shaped — like a monster mushroom. There are people with skin all shrivelled from the burns. Some of them are kids. There is smoke and fire everywhere. I swallow and swallow and swallow to keep from crying. How can people possibly think that dropping that bomb was the right thing to do?

"That's how hell must be," whispers Sandra.

Aunt Bette puts her hand on Sandra's shoulder.

"The hell we humans make right here on earth, is the only kind of hell I believe in darlin,' though others in our church would disagree." She looks so sad.

In another book I read that the Americans dropped another bomb three days later — on Nagasaki, another Japanese city. I can't believe that they did it all over again. I feel sick.

Suddenly I can't figure out why the United States was fighting Japan in the first place. "I thought the war was against Hitler in Germany — not against Japan," I say.

"It tells about that in this book," says Sandra. She points to a section in a World War II book. It says that Japan and Germany were both fighting the U.S. But Germany had already surrendered when they dropped the atom bomb on Hiroshima. Mr. Truman, who was President then, thought that dropping the bomb might make Japan surrender, too.

About Sadako, though, we don't really find out more than we already know. We show the *Current Events Newsletter* article to the librarian. The *Newsletter* says that Sadako's story was taken from Japanese newspapers — one called *Hokkaido Shimbun* and one called *Chugoku Shimbun*. But the library doesn't have those newspapers, and they'd be written in Japanese anyway. "Disappointing, but you may have to go on what you already know about Sadako," says Aunt Bette.

"I wish we knew how to make that bird," says Sandra. She points to a picture of a folded paper crane beside the *Current Events Newsletter* story.

"Why, darlin', what a clever idea," says Aunt Bette. Sandra's sad face turns into a smile. Aunt Bette holds Sandra's face between her hands and says, "You are totally transformed when you smile."

"This huge library must have books about how to make the birds," I say. "Let's go ask."

The librarian looks at the picture of the folded bird. "Origami," she says. "A Japanese paper-folding art. I'll show you the origami books." She marches ahead of us and finds a book with pictures that show how to make paper cranes.

We leave the library with a few kids' books about World War II, the magazine with the awful pictures, and the origami book.

"Time to reward our hard work with some restaurant food," says Aunt Bette.

"Whoop-de-do and hallelujah!" But all at once I feel ashamed — like maybe I'm not supposed to have fun because of Sadako and the bomb and stuff.

It's already dark when we leave the library. There are lights all over the place, blinking and twinkling. Aunt Bette says they're called neon lights. Some of the neon lights move in circles that go around and around the signs. The lights bedazzle me. Is bedazzle a word? It doesn't matter. That's how I feel. Bedazzled. Except that those awful magazine pictures keep buzzing about in my brain, spoiling my bedazzlement. The neon signs just keep blinking. They don't even care. I try to erase the terrible pictures from my head, just for now.

"Drive slowly," I say to Aunt Bette. "I want to see it all." I look this way and that, as fast as I can. Sandra's eyes are big. "Isn't this great, Sandra?" I ask.

"I guess so, but ..."

"But what?"

"I don't know … I'm too sad about the bomb. And Mamma says … um … to live simply." Sandra's mamma is always trying to make Sandra's life boring, even more than my mamma. Maybe these lights are part of the temptations Mamma was worried about. I admit, I'm feeling tempted to come back to Wichita again, maybe sometime when I don't have to look up awful stuff at the library.

And then we get to the restaurant.

"Hi, Walter," says Aunt Bette as we walk in. She *knows* the guy at the restaurant.

"It's always nice to see you, Bette. And who are these two charming young ladies?"

We both blush as Aunt Bette introduces us. Nobody ever said I was charming before in my whole life. Walter leads us to a table that has a blue table cloth and a red candle right smack in the middle. A waiter comes with menus. He lights the candle. I feel as glowy as the candle, until I remember those awful bomb pictures. Again, I try to put that out of my head.

The menus are so long. There's steak and pork chops and fish, and a gazillion other things. I could stay here all night just choosing. I finally decide on salmon because we hardly ever have fish at our house. There aren't many lakes around where we live.

"Enjoy your dinner," says the waiter.

When he leaves, I ask Aunt Bette, "How come he calls supper, 'dinner?'"

"Some folks call the evening meal dinner," she says.

I notice that the waiter is talking to the people at the table right next to ours. What if he heard? When he passes our table he winks at me. "We city folks are so confused. We don't know the difference between dinner and supper." My face is probably permanently pink from blushing so often. But the waiter looks so friendly that I don't really mind his teasing. I smile at him.

The salmon is yummy, the restaurant feels all cozy, and I love being here with Aunt Bette and Sandra — but those horrible bomb pictures keep pushing into my head. Sadako will never get to go to a restaurant. Her piece of forever was so short.

When we're finished, the waiter asks, "How about one of our fine desserts?" Sandra and I look at Aunt Bette.

"Well, I'd say we definitely need a finishing touch." Looking at Sandra and me, she says, "Besides, how could I resist your big, shining eyes?" She turns back to the waiter. "What are the choices?"

"Perhaps you'd like to come to our dessert display and make a choice."

We go to a counter with yummy-looking desserts behind glass. There are pies and cakes with fluffy whipped cream and red cherries and all stuff like that.

Oh, my! How am I going to choose?

I'm about to point to a chocolate cake with a pink, custardy filling. But then I see a fluffy pink cake with a strawberry filling. I can't make up my mind. It reminds me of the time I was at an ice cream store when I was about five, and there were about a thousand different kinds to choose from. Mamma kept saying stuff like, "Hurry and make up your mind" and "We have to go home and milk the cows." I hate hurrying up. Hate it, hate it, hate it! I can't think when I'm hurrying. "I can't decide," I say to the waiter. All at once I feel shy and ashamed, and five-years-old again.

"Take your time," he says.

"We're in no rush," says Aunt Bette. I'm so glad and ... relieved — yes, that's the word, relieved — about not having to hurry, that tears spring to my eyes. I put my arms around Aunt Bette's waist. I wouldn't dare put my arms around the waiter's waist. I finally choose the pink cake with strawberry filling. Sandra points to a white cake with white icing.

"What?" I say. "You want something that looks that boring?" Oops! I turn to the waiter. I feel the fiery embarrassment on my face again. "Sorry, I didn't mean ..." I'm probably not charming anymore.

But he just laughs. "It's okay. Though our pineapple-vanilla cake may not be quite as interesting to look at, it has a very fine taste. Is that what you'd like, miss?"

"Um ..." Sandra looks at another cake with shiny cherry topping.

"Of course," says the waiter, "the cherry-glazed chiffon is also a very fine choice."

Sandra smiles and chooses the cherry-glazed chiffon. But at the table, she just stares at her dessert. "Sadako can't eat cake ever again," she says.

Aunt Bette has a fork full of chocolate cake halfway to her mouth. She puts it down.

"I was thinking stuff like that too," I say. "Like maybe I shouldn't have fun because Sadako can't ... and how can we just sit here and have a good time after seeing those horrible pictures?"

"Yeah!" says Sandra in a voice much bigger than her usual voice.

Aunt Bette looks back and forth between Sandra and me. "A cloud has been passing over your faces every few bites. Will the two of you being miserable help Sadako in any way?" Sandra and I look at each other. "Will it undo the horror of the bomb if you refuse to eat cherry-glazed cake?" That sounds so silly that I laugh. Sandra

97

has a tiny red-faced smile. "Oh darlin's ..." Aunt Bette puts one hand over my hand, and the other over Sandra's. Her eyes are soft. "What the world needs is joy. We need to bring happiness into the world."

"Aunt Bette likes to speechify and preachify," I say to Sandra.

"You better believe it," says Aunt Bette, "and I'm not finished yet. All we know about Sadako says that she was a spunky, spirited girl. Think about what that says about how we should live our lives."

"You finished preachifying?"

"Almost. I just want you to know how proud I am of the two of you. Your project shows how much you do care."

I sigh a glad sigh. In this piece of forever I'm going to enjoy this piece of cake. I take a bite. So does Sandra. *Um-yummy!*

As we leave the restaurant, our waiter says to me, "Did you enjoy your cherry-glazed chiffon?" Sandra and I look at each other.

"It was Sandra who had the cherry-glazed

chiffon," I say. "Not me. You city folks are so confused." Oh, dear, that was probably rude. But Aunt Bette and the waiter both laugh big, booming laughs.

12

Something Important in the World

The next morning Cindy stands near me. She glances at me. I pretend I don't notice. But again I wonder if she wants to make up and be friends. But she doesn't say anything, and neither do I.

When the bell rings, Mr. Foster puts a letter on my desk. "It's from Mr. Lambert." My belly does a flip-flop. I don't even want to open it. He'll think I'm chicken for sure. My fingers fumble and tremble as I open the letter.

Dear Rose,

Thank you for the invitation to the Veterans Day assembly. I will come. I am befuddled in my mind about war, too ...

My mouth hangs open. I am so amazed.

... though I surely was proud and full of enthusi-
asm when I enlisted.

I put the letter down for a couple of seconds to
think about this.

I liked your thoughtful letter. I certainly do not
think you or your papa are chicken. It is very
brave to stand up for what you believe. Especially
when you are going against popular opinion.

He thinks we're *brave!* I stare at those words,
smiling through watery eyes.

"I take it you got a good letter from Mr.
Lambert," says Mr. Foster.

"Um ... yes, sir. He's coming to the Veterans
Day assembly." I'm mad at Mr. Foster though.
He butted right into a private moment between
me and Mr. Lambert.

"I'm glad he's coming," says Mr. Foster.

I go back to the letter.

And no, I didn't know about Sadako. When
innocent people die, it makes me sad and angry
too.

Mr. Lambert has so many of the same thoughts as
I have. I can hardly believe it.

> *I think you must be a creative and courageous*
> *young woman, and I'm sure you will do some-*
> *thing important in the world.*

Something important in the world? I stare and stare
at those words.

> *The death of your animals does count. All life*
> *counts. I had a dog once — name of Spot. The*
> *day Spot died was one of the saddest days of*
> *my life.*

> *With respect, AJ Lambert*

With respect. No one has ever said — or written —
those words to me before in my whole life. Kids
forever have to respect their elders, but don't get
respected back. I let Mr. Lambert's words lie
warm in my belly. This is the best letter ever.

"Have you finished your math, Rose?" asks
Mr. Foster.

"Not yet, Mr. Foster." I take out my math workbook. Who wants to do stupid math? I just want to
think about the letter and about doing something
important in the world. Something brave.

*   *   *

At my house after school Sandra and I fold paper

102

cranes for our project. She figures out the instructions real quick. And almost right away she is making good cranes. My first ones are all wiggly-squiggly. The birds have to be folded exactly right, from the start. Otherwise they get more and more lopsided. But I finally get the hang of it. "This is so much fun," I say.

"But it's because of Sadako ..." says Sandra. She stops. "Oh, I forgot. It won't help Sadako if we're sad." She smiles.

I grin at her. "Yeah, being grumpy and sour-faced won't help."

For our project we're going to tell about the bombs in Japan, and show the pictures, even though they're horrible. And of course we'll tell about Sadako. But the fun part — the 'artistic component' — will be showing the kids how to make the cranes.

After supper I practice my Sadako report on our steps. I'm saying it out loud. I've barely started when Daniel crawls out from the space under the steps. Oh, no! I should have checked under the steps before I started. He probably heard. I said the part about Sadako dying because of the bomb. I would never have told Daniel on purpose. His eyes are going back and forth, and his forehead has worried, scrunchy lines. I know he's about to ask a gazillion questions.

"What's a Sadako?" He heard, all right.

"Sadako is ... um ... was a girl in Japan."

"Did Sadako get dead, wike the bird?"

"Yes, Daniel." I put my arms around him.

"And ... and ... did the sod-ier drop the bomb on top of Sadako?"

I sigh. "In a war, soldiers drop bombs out of the airplane onto the enemy."

"What's an em ... em-en-y?"

"Not em-en-y, Daniel. En-em-y. Well, that's who you fight because ... uh ..."

"... because you don't wike your emeny?" He still gets the word wrong. "Didn't the so-dier *wike* Sadako?" He looks completely befuddled.

"Well ..." How can I explain it when I don't understand it either? "Uh ... he wasn't mad at Sadako exactly, but he was trying to win a war so ... um ... he dropped the bomb and some people were ... uh ... killed." I don't tell him that thousands of people were killed. I also don't tell him the part about how Sadako didn't seem hurt at first, but died later. It's just too complicated for a little kid.

Daniel's eyes are big. "But ... but ... did the sodier's mamma *know* that he dropped the bomb on top of Sadako?"

"I don't know." But inside myself, there is something I do know, and I say it out loud to Daniel. "I don't believe in bombs ... or war."

"I don't either. It makes peep-o get dead."

I sit on the steps a long time thinking about stuff. I read that President Truman decided to drop the bomb. Maybe this idea started out being just a tiny thought in his head. But then that tiny thought turned into something big and horrible. That tiny piece of forever turned into a huge, horrible hunk of forever. But then another thought pops into my head. Maybe ... a tiny, *good* thought could turn into a big, giant, wonderful thing. That thought cheers me up.

I also think about Mr. Lambert's letter.

Especially the part about being brave and doing something important in the world. He said speaking up for what we believe is brave. What if I spoke up about Sadako at the Veterans Day assembly? No, I could never do that. But what if this teeny-tiny thought, about speaking out at assembly, turned into something much bigger? No, I won't even think about it anymore, because Mr. Foster would never *ever* let me.

I'm still sitting on the steps in the almost-dark when I see Zippy. I wonder if he'll ever get completely tamed, like Dancer. I call out to him. He isn't all crouched and scared looking like he used to be, so there's hope. I think of going into the kitchen for milk, but decide I don't have to feed him every single time. Anyway, he's not so skinny anymore. "Maybe someday you'll sit on my lap. If you feel like it." He sits down, watching me. He's only a couple of feet away.

13

Something Horribly Wrong

I know something is horribly wrong when I walk
into the schoolroom. A big sadness hangs in the
air. Kids glance at Judy's desk. It is empty. It is
so-o-o quiet. Even Mr. Foster doesn't say anything for awhile. Everyone looks so serious, as if
someone died or something. All at once my belly
lurches. What if ... I look again at Judy's empty
desk. Mr. Foster is still just standing there. He
swallows a couple of times. His Adam's apple goes
up and down. It looks sort of funny, but I push
that thought away real quick. Not a time for
thinking such things.

Everybody's eyes are glued to Mr. Foster. In
the middle of the quiet, someone's desk creaks.

Finally Mr. Foster says, "Boys and girls, I have some very sad news. Judy ..."

What if Judy ...? The feeling in my belly moves to my throat. I swallow a few times. Maybe my Adam's apple is doing funny things, too. But I don't have a big, bulgy one like Mr. Foster. Why can't I make myself stop looking at his bobbing Adam's apple?

"... Judy's dad, Mr. Kline, has died." Oh! I sigh a big sigh. I'm glad it isn't Judy. In just a tiny space of time, a bunch of thoughts churn around in my head. Even though Judy has been awful to me lately, I'm glad she didn't die. And I'm glad that I'm glad. I would feel terrible if I wanted her to die. And, all this time, I just can't help noticing that Mr. Foster's Adam's apple is bobbing up and down like mad. How can I be thinking about a stupid Adam's apple at a time like this? I feel like laughing and crying at the same time.

Tom raises his hand. "Mr. Foster," he asks in a small voice, "How did Judy's papa die?"

Again Mr. Foster is quiet for awhile. Finally he says, "That is another hard thing. But Mrs.

Kline — she is a brave woman — doesn't want to hide the truth. Mr. Kline took his own life. He shot himself." Kids gasp. Some start sobbing. My eyes fill up, too.

Mr. Foster swallows once, then goes on. "Mr. Kline fought in the most recent war — the Korean War. He has been ... troubled ever since his return. The recent wars have been tough on all of us who fought, and have family who ... fought." His voice gets quiet and even a little wobbly, like that day when he was going to tell us about the current events project but then told us to do silent reading instead. "We don't know yet when the funeral will be." There are big spaces between everything Mr. Foster says. "We will have a special time to remember Mr. Kline during our Veterans Day assembly." Again he stops, then adds, "Judy will need our kindness."

At recess, a kid named Norman glares at me. "See how hard it is for people who were *brave* and went to war! Not like some people who stayed safe the whole time." He turns and runs before I have time to answer. Norman is a kid who hasn't said nasty stuff to me before. I sure don't need more kids bugging me. Suddenly I feel tired. Just tired. Tired of trying to stand up to kids. Of trying to figure out how to be brave.

After school I sneak off to Grandmother Oak before doing my chores. I snuggle into my cozy spot as best I can, though I don't fit into the space as well as I used to. *It's not my fault — or Papa's fault — about Judy's papa.* It seems like Norman was blaming us. I want to yell and scream, but Mamma is in the garden. If she hears a peep out of me, she'll make me come right down. It's the war's fault. If Judy's papa hadn't been in the war, maybe he wouldn't have been so troubled, and wouldn't have killed himself. War troubles me, too, and I wasn't even in one. Before I know it, I'm crying for lots of reasons. Because of Judy's papa — *what if my papa had died?* — because of my friends turning against me, because of the horrible bomb on Hiroshima, because of Sadako. *Sadako!* Thoughts about Judy's papa and Sadako are getting all mixed together in my head. I think hard about them both. There's something that's trying to push into my head, but I can't quite figure out what it is.

That evening we visit Judy and her mamma. Daniel stays with Aunt Bette. I'm nervous. What will I say to Judy? She probably doesn't even want me to come.

My heart is thumpity-bumping as we knock on the door. Judy's mamma opens the door. Her eyes are puffy. "Good of you to come," she says.

Mamma hands her some fresh cinnamon rolls that she baked. Then she stands stiffly. "I'm so sorry ..."

I throw my arms around Judy's mamma, maybe because Mamma doesn't. I hadn't planned to hug her. It kind of happened by itself. Maybe my arms know what to do even if my head doesn't. Judy's mamma smiles a sad smile at me. She touches my cheek. I like her.

In the house there is a bunch of other folks. And food on a table — cookies and stuff. Judy is sitting by herself. I go to her. Now what? A hug sure doesn't happen this time. I sit down. Anything I say would probably sound dumb. I don't say anything. Neither does she. She has a kind of "nothing" look on her face — blank. Doesn't even let on that she knows I'm there. The grown-ups are talking in low, droning voices. Some are sobbing. Nearly all the women are holding handkerchiefs. There is nose-blowing and eye-dabbing. I wish I were somewhere else.

Cindy comes with her mamma. She goes to sit on the other side of Judy. Judy moves closer to Cindy — away from me. Suddenly I'm mad. I know I'm only supposed to think kind thoughts about Judy at a time like this. But that bad feeling just crept into me when Judy moved away from me. *I'm doing the best I can.*

*　　*　　*

That night, when I'm almost asleep, all at once my eyes fly open because a thought pops into my head. It's what was trying to push into my head when I was with Grandmother Oak. Judy's papa and Sadako both didn't have an injury, so folks thought they were all right. But bad stuff was going on inside both of them. For Sadako it was the atom-bomb sickness, and for Judy's papa it was the awful stuff he remembered. And then, years later they both died because of the war. So that's the part that is the same about how they died. But a part that's different is that Sadako wanted to live, and Judy's papa didn't anymore. The war was a piece of his forever that was just too hard. I stay awake a long time thinking about Judy's papa. It's so sad when people don't want to live. And because he was so sad — and killed himself — Judy and her mamma are real sad. Sadness makes more sadness, like violence makes more violence.

And I think about how I sometimes wondered if Judy's papa was mean to her. He did talk real mean to her sometimes when he picked her up from school. I don't know if we're supposed to think only good stuff about someone when they're dead, but how can I just push the bad parts away? Anyway, maybe now I understand better why he wasn't very nice sometimes.

*   *   *

The funeral is a couple of days later. The tiny Methodist church is only about half full. Maybe

113

Judy's family doesn't have many friends. The service is a blur of songs, Bible readings, prayers, and stuff led by Reverend Jewett.

"Yea though I walk through the valley of the shadow of death ..."

"We pay our respects to this man who fought for freedom and democracy."

Papa wants to work for freedom and democracy, too. So do I.

More words, more prayers, more songs.

"Shall we gather at the river ..."

We file out of the church. Somehow I have to get past Judy, who is standing with her mamma at the door. "I'm sorry," I say to her in an almost-whisper. She pretends she doesn't hear.

Outside, a meadowlark on a telephone line sings his three-note song. He doesn't even care that a man is dead.

14

The Yummiest Crumb

The first day Judy comes back to school after her papa died, the kids kind of glance at her, then look away — like they're scared of her or something. I admit it's hard to know what to say to someone whose papa just died. Especially since he killed himself. But during lunch time I almost feel sorry about the kids ignoring her. I actually think about going to her. But she would never want to talk to me.

I open my lunch pail. Oh, yummy! I have a big, fat cinnamon roll that Mamma baked. She makes the best cinnamon rolls ever! I look at the cinnamon roll. I look at Judy. All at once my crazy feet walk to Judy. "You want a piece of my cinnamon roll?"

"Stay away from me," she yells. "I don't want you, or any of your yellow-bellied, Nazi-loving family near me. Your papa stayed safe the whole time and my papa ..." She doesn't finish the sentence. "And I sure don't want your *stupid* cinnamon roll." She stomps away.

My face burns. I bite my bottom lip to keep it from trembling. But I don't hang my head. I don't say anything to Judy. But inside my head I yell, *I'll never, ever be nice to you again!*

All the kids are really quiet. Some are staring at the ground. Others glance back and forth from me to Judy. Finally Tom says, "I'd sure like a piece of your cinnamon roll." I look at Tom to make sure he's serious. He's smiling. The air around me seems to breathe again. I give him a piece.

"Thanks. Yummm." He smacks his lips.

I grin at him. Suddenly I feel all relieved. Words pop out of my mouth. "Who else wants a piece?" Sandra comes over. I give her a piece. Other kids look at Tom. They look at my big, fat cinnamon roll with icing slathered all over it. And suddenly everyone gathers around me —

except Cindy and, of course, Judy, who is hunched by herself on the schoolhouse steps. I have a big hurt in my guts that Cindy doesn't come. She looks sort of sad. But I'm sure not going to beg her to eat *my* food.

The others say how good the cinnamon roll is. Of course, everyone gets only a tiny piece by the time I share it out. It reminds me of communion in church. That's when all the grown-ups get a small piece of bread that is a symbol of Jesus' body. But at church I feel left out, because us kids don't get any. Anyway, I pop the last teeny-tiny piece into my mouth — just a crumb actually. I grin at the kids. "This is the yummiest crumb I've ever eaten." Everyone laughs. I feel almost happy, but not quite, because Cindy is still mad at me. And some tiny corner of my brain feels bad for Judy, who is still hunched by herself on the schoolhouse steps.

Back in the schoolhouse, that tiny part of my brain grows a wee bit bigger.

Judy's papa just died, says a voice in my head.

Another voice says, *Yeah, but I tried to be nice to*

117

her and she just yelled at me.

The two voices in my head keep yammering at each other.

When people have a big sadness in their life, sometimes that makes them say or do nasty things.

But she's always been nasty.

Be quiet! I say to the arguing voices in my head. I have work to do. I fold some more cranes for our project.

Sandra and I have a whole pile of cranes — red ones, blue ones, yellow ones. The one I like best of all is a little polka-dotted green one that I made from Christmas wrapping paper. I'll find a special place for it in my room when our project is over. We're going to decorate the whole classroom with hanging cranes for our presentation. Kids keep looking at us, and at the cranes. Even Judy glances over every once in a while. Cindy, too.

At recess everyone crowds around us except Judy and Cindy.

"Can I help?" says Tom. He has been so nice to me lately. Sometimes, in my secret thoughts, I imagine that I am Anne of Green Gables, and Tom is Gilbert Blythe. Tom looks real good — for a boy. He has black, curly hair and blue eyes.

"But you have your own project," I say.

"Yeah, but I don't mind helping. Will you show me how to fold those?"

"Sure."

But Mr. Foster says, "Go outside. It's recess."

Sandra and I move to the schoolhouse steps, taking some paper for the cranes. Judy runs off. "Who wants to make stupid old birds?" she says. Tom and lots of the kids stay on the steps while Sandra and I try to show them how to fold the cranes. But Tom's fingers are clumsy, and he soon gives up and goes to play ball. Other kids want to play ball too.

"Don't worry," says Sandra. "We'll show you how when we do our project." When they hear that, they run off to the ball field. Only Sandra and I are left folding.

Everyone else is playing ball — except Cindy. She sits on a swing a little ways from us — not swinging much, just sitting there, pretending not to be interested in what we're doing.

"Cindy, come play ball," yells Tom.

"Nah, I don't feel like it today."

I glance at her, but she quickly looks away. She swirls the swing around so that the chain above her twists. Then she lifts her feet and the swing twirls, round and, round. I see all this from the corner of my eye. Cindy would be really good at making cranes, I bet. She has patience with stuff that takes lots of time. Should I ask her if she wants to? No, I'm too afraid.

Before I can stop myself, I glance at her again. Again she quickly looks away. This is so embarrassing. I *won't* look again. But the corner of my eye sees that she does twirly swirls on the swing again. The corner of my eye is so busy. I do wish we were friends again. *You want to come fold cranes, Cindy?* But I can't make the words come out of my mouth.

The bell rings. Recess is over. Suddenly I know what to do. I take my most special crane, the little polka-dotted green one. I walk to the swing. Seeing me, Cindy stares into her lap.

What if she doesn't take the crane? What if she yells at me? I put the crane in her lap, then turn and walk away. I feel like running, in case she yells at me or something, but I make myself walk, as if I'm not scared. But I'm all trembly.

After school, I sit on the school steps tying a shoestring that has come undone. Cindy comes and sits beside me. She doesn't say anything for a while. Now it's me staring down. My shoe is tied, but I keep fiddling with the string. I do a double knot, and Cindy still doesn't say anything. Should I get up and leave or what? Finally she says, "Um ... I like the bird." I feel like crying. "Will you show me how to make the birds?"

"Yeah," I say in a choky voice.

Then she says, "I'm sorry about ... um ... you know, what I said to you about what my papa said. I wasn't gonna tell you those horrible words, but that day when you yelled at me, I got mad ... and those words flew out of my mouth, sort of."

I don't know what to say to her. Finally I say, "Yeah, I sure did yell that day. I'm sorry, too." Then I add, "Angry stuff flies out of my mouth lots of times." We both laugh, and the giggles feel good. "But I sure wish your papa didn't think that stuff."

"Me too," she says.

15

Stuck With You

I can't believe it. Mr. Foster is making Judy be in the Sadako project with Sandra and me. Judy never did get started on a project, even though most kids are nearly done with theirs. It's understandable, though, with Judy's papa dying and all. Anyway, because all the other kids are already in groups of three, Mr. Foster said she had to be with us.

At recess, everyone bursts out the door.

"You ain't nothin' but a hound dog," croons Tom. The kids have all been belting out Elvis Presley songs lately, jiggling their hips like he does.

Judy wiggle-waggles her way up to me. *"You ain't nothin' but a chicken,"* she sings in a snooty voice. "Guess I'm stuck with you *chickens*." She makes chicken sounds. "Guess I'm gonna have to join your stupid project and make those stupid birds."

A boiling in my belly almost burbles right out of my mouth. *Guess we're stuck with* you! I stop myself, but my thoughts still rage. *And how dare you call the birds stupid? They are symbols of peace.* Uh-oh. I sure don't feel peaceful now. An Elvis song pops into my head and saves me. I look Judy straight in the eye, wiggle-waggle as hard as I can, and croon, *"Don't be cruel."*

The kids laugh, Tom hardest of all. And, oh, it feels good. Cindy grins. Maybe I got my spunk back. Maybe I never lost it.

Judy huffs, "You think you're so smart." She must feel bad, because of the kids laughing. I know what that feels like.

"I'll show you how to make the cranes," Sandra says to Judy. Sandra is nicer than I am. She's trying to help Judy feel better, even though Judy was nasty. I respect Sandra more than I used to. I like that word *respect*. Mr. Lambert said it in his letter. He respects me, and I respect Sandra. Maybe there's hope for me.

Sandra shows Judy how to fold the cranes.

"That's real good," she says, even though Judy's first crane is all crooked.

"You thought I wouldn't be good at it?" Her voice is still nasty. Can't she ever say anything nice? But there is a tiny smile on the corner of her lips. She makes more and more cranes. And after a while, she's quiet — for once. She bites her bottom lip as she concentrates. I remember how she kept sneaking looks when Sandra and I were folding all those cranes. Maybe Judy is happy that Mr. Foster made her be in our project, because now she can pretend she's only making cranes because she has to.

As we fold cranes, a thought pops out of my mouth. "What do you think of doing our project at the Veterans Day assembly, and not only for our class?" I had this thought once before, and had pushed the idea away. "Of course we'd have to ask Mr. Foster." Even as I say this, I think he would never let us.

Sandra stares at me. "That would never work."

"Why not?" I ask. "It would be brave."

"It would be dumb!" Every once in awhile, Sandra's voice is louder than it used to be. Judy keeps looking back and forth between Sandra and me. Then Sandra says, more quietly, "I don't think it would help peace at all. It would only make folks mad, because ... um ... our project is about how war is wro —" She looks at Judy. "I mean ... our project is about the horrible things that happen in war, and the Veterans Day program is about ... how soldiers fight, and about thanking veterans ... for their service."

"You don't want to thank veterans?" Judy is angry again. Sandra looks confused. She doesn't say anything.

Should I say something? After a while I say, "I think the veterans were very brave, and I'm really sorry about everybody who died. Especially ... um ... your papa." Judy stares into her lap. We are all quiet. As we sit, I wonder if Judy feels like she's not an important part of the project, since she joined so late. "Do you have ideas for the project, Judy?" I ask.

She looks surprised. Then she gets a thinking look — she scrunches her forehead. "Yeah, I got an idea. Maybe we can make one of these bird things for every single person who comes."

Sandra and I stare at her.

"Yeah," says Sandra.

"That's such a great idea," I say.

"You didn't think I could have a good idea?"

Accch! My burble belly boils again, but inside my head I know what Judy said is true. I *am* kind of surprised that she has a good idea. Out loud I say, "Like Judy said, we can just give out the cranes at the Veterans Day assembly. We don't have to do our whole project. We can say the cranes mean we hope that someday there won't be wars. *Everyone* will agree with *that*." Judy smiles — a real, across-her-whole-face smile.

Later, I ask Mr. Foster about giving out cranes. He agrees to it. He also agrees that I can say a sentence that the cranes mean we hope someday there won't be wars. "But if you say more than that, Rose, it might be ... ah ... awkward."

But suddenly I wonder if one sentence is *really* enough. "Uh, Mr. Foster, how will the people know *why* cranes are a symbol of peace, unless I tell them just a *teeny-tiny* bit about Sadako."

"One sentence, Rose!" he says in a don't-argue-with-me voice. I know it's useless to say anything else about it.

Over the next few days we make a gazillion cranes for Veterans Day. Cindy helps, too, even though she's not in our project. I'm so glad we're friends again.

16

Little Boy and Fat Man

"On a sunny day, August 6, 1945, the United States dropped an atom bomb on Hiroshima, a city in Japan." My heart pitter-patters as I start my project report. I don't like talking about stuff so awful. And what if the kids get mad at me all over again? But I keep going.

"About 70,000 people died right away." Some kids gasp. "And thousands more died later from injuries, especially horrible burns, and also from atom-bomb sickness."

Norman raises his hand. "I thought we were supposed to do our projects on something that's happening right now."

"Um ... well, because of the bomb, some people

are still dying right now in 1956.

"No way," says Norman.

"The bomb caused something called radiation, which made lots of people sick later. These people were far enough from the bomb so that they didn't have an injury at first. But later they got atom-bomb sickness ... from the radiation."

I go back to my report. "Anyway, the U.S. Air Force dropped the bomb because they hoped it would make Japan surrender, and the war would end sooner. Germany had already surrendered. The bomb was called Little Boy." Some kids snicker — nervous snickers, like maybe they're not supposed to laugh.

"But what happened was not little. Little Boy made huge, horrible ... um, destruction." I show them a couple of magazine pictures — of the fiery mushroom cloud and the city all smashed. The kids aren't laughing anymore. Their eyes are big. "Little Boy was dropped right smack in the middle of Hiroshima and flattened just about everything. And the people — where the bomb was dropped — didn't even have a chance." I stop.

Just talking about it makes the back of my eyes sting. And I don't feel like showing more pictures. The kids already look so horrified. "I was going to show you more pictures but ... I don't know ..."

"Show us," whispers Cindy.

"Yeah," says Tom, "We're in fifth grade. We have to know."

For once Mr. Foster doesn't stop the kids from talking out, even though they didn't raise their hands.

I show them more pictures, even the one with the little boy about Daniel's age, crying beside a dead woman. Every time I see that picture I have a sniffle-sob in my throat. Everyone looks sadder than sad. A few of the girls sniffle a little. I almost can't bear to tell them the next part.

"A few days later, on August 9, the U.S. Air Force dropped another bomb — on Nagasaki."

"What?"

"Why?"

This time Mr. Foster stops them. "We'll ask questions later."

"I couldn't believe it either," I say. "That they

did it again. This bomb was called Fat Man."

Some more guilty smirks.

"After the first bomb, Mr. Truman — he was President then — said if Japan didn't surrender right away, there'd be another bomb. Fat Man killed about 40,000 people right away, and many more died later. After that, Japan surrendered."

When I'm finished, the kids ask questions. Some of their questions I've already answered in my report, but I tell them again.

"I don't get it," says Norman. "Why did the U.S. drop the bombs?"

"Like I said, some people thought it would end the war quicker."

"Did it?"

"Yes, I guess so. But I still think it was a horrible, horrible thing to do. And I read that our President Eisenhower — he was a General then — thought that Japan was ready to surrender anyway, so he didn't want to drop the bomb."

"But how come they did it *again*, with Fat Man?" asks Tom.

"People don't agree about that." I try to

remember all the stuff I read. "Some said they had to do it so Japan would surrender *immediately*. Other people said that they wanted to see which of the two bombs worked better ..." *Worked better*? *What am I saying*? "I mean which one ..."

"... killed more people?" asks Tom.

"I guess so." I'm almost whispering. That's too horrible. "Anyway, Fat Man was made with some different stuff than Little Boy. Fat Man had um ... plu — " I look at my notes. "... plutonium."

After my part, Sandra tells the story about Sadako. About how she was far enough away from the bomb so that she didn't seem hurt at first. How she used to run in competitions for her school. How ten years later Sadako got sick after all, because of the radiation. How a Japanese legend said that folding 1,000 cranes would make a sick person well. How Sadako folded paper cranes, but died anyway. How lots of people are still getting sick from the bomb. And how a statue is being built *right now* in Hiroshima's Peace Park.

Sandra ends by saying, "The statue is so we remember Sadako and all the children who died because of the bomb. Sadako didn't do anything wrong against the Americans. She didn't even throw one teeny-tiny stone. Just like lots of other Japanese kids — and grown-ups — who didn't do anything wrong. So why did Sadako and the others have to die?"

After Sandra's part, Judy shows how to fold the cranes, though a few kids already know. Judy is now good at folding, but she isn't very good at explaining. Those of us who already know how go around helping the others. Still, there's a big confusing muddle of questions and crooked cranes. But we keep folding. We have to have enough for the Veterans Day assembly.

As we make the cranes, kids talk about Sadako and the bomb.

"I don't believe in the atom bomb," says one kid.

"I don't either," says another, "but I believe in other kinds of war — like fighting with guns and stuff."

"Don't you believe in *any* kind of war?" Tom asks me.

"No."

And nobody says I'm chicken or anything.

* * *

I sit against the trunk of Grandmother Oak. Stinker is in my lap, purring. Zippy is here, too. He's not very close to me, but he doesn't look even one tiny bit afraid. And I don't have to be so careful every single minute about not scaring him — like not moving too quickly, or not talking too loudly. "Our presentation went really well," I say to the cats. But Stinker knows something is still bothering me. She licks my hand, like she's trying to help me feel better. Zippy just sits there, licking his paws. He doesn't care about my worries. I pick up a twig and draw a sad face in the dirt. Thoughts spin in my head — about Sadako, and about the Veterans Day assembly tomorrow. "Do you think I'll do something important in the world, Zippy?" I ask. "Do you think I'm brave enough?"

17

Veterans Day Assembly

"Oh say can you see
By the dawn's early light ..."
I'm belting it out as loudly as anyone else — the
first song of the Veterans Day assembly, our
national anthem.

"What so proudly we hail
In the twilight's last gleaming ..."
I feel all shivery.

"And the rocket's red glare
The bombs bursting in air ..."
The bombs bursting in air. I stop singing. The
song makes it sound like watching firecrackers at
a picnic. I think of the Hiroshima bomb. But it's
our *national anthem*. What if thinking thoughts

against our national anthem is like ... blasphemy, or something. And the tune sounds so happy. And the air feels almost electric.

Then Cindy sings a verse all by herself. She sings really well. As we sing, Tom comes down the aisle passing out red paper poppies. Should I take one? If I do, does it mean I believe in war? Well, it's not like I have time to figure it out, and if I don't take one, the kids will think I don't even care about the dead soldiers. I take one. I look at Sandra. She doesn't take one. She stares at the poppy in my hand. She glares at me. I pin on my poppy and glare right back. But my hands tremble. The truth is, my whole body feels trembly.

Tom goes up front. "I will recite *In Flanders Fields* by John McCrae, a Canadian soldier who fought in World War I," he says. "Though this is a World War I poem, it has meaning for any war."

"*In Flanders Fields the poppies blow
Between the crosses, row on row ...*"
The words make a big lump in my throat.

"*That mark our place; and in the sky
The larks, still bravely singing, fly*

Scarce heard amid the guns below."
There is a big sadness in my belly, and I can feel it in the whole room.

"We are the Dead. Short days ago
We lived, felt dawn, saw sunset glow ..."
Short days ago Judy's papa lived.

"Loved, and were loved, and now we lie,
In Flanders Fields."
People are sniffling. Even me.

The veterans are sitting on stage facing us. There's one really old guy who scowls out at us. He probably was in World War I. Actually, he looks sort of like Uncle Sam — skinny, with a pointy nose. There's one other scowling guy. He has black eyebrows that almost run together in the middle. He is wearing a uniform with bars and medals and stuff. Maybe that one is Cindy's papa. I don't want to think about that. It will only make me more nervous. But a picture pops into my head of him chasing me out of the school-house, and he keeps chasing and chasing until he runs me right out of the country.

My heart thumps and I can't make it stop. I'm

so nervous, even though I only have one sentence to say at the end. To help myself feel better, I try to figure out which one is Mr. Lambert. Some are wearing ordinary clothes instead of uniforms, even farmers' clothing. Somehow I think Mr. Lambert might be one of those.

There are lots of songs, prayers, and speeches. Lots of standing up and sitting down, like church calisthenics. Mr. Bain, our principal, gets up between each part to tell what will happen next. And there are lots of words, like *valiant war heroes ... our brave men in uniform ... died for a great and glorious cause ... protect our freedom and democracy.* And inside my head I know I want to work for freedom and democracy, too, to protect people like Sadako, even if I have to die for what I believe. But I don't know yet how I'll do that. Maybe there could be an army for peace — with no guns. *I will be brave.*

There is a special part of the program just for Judy's papa. Judy and her mamma have a place in the front row. Mr. Bain says, "Though we are here to pay tribute to all our veterans, we especially want to remember Mr. Kline, who served in the Korean War. The emotional impact of this war took a great toll on Mr. Kline, and today we pay special respect to him." Mr. Bain introduces Reverend Jewett, who does some prayers and Bible readings and stuff, like he did at the funeral. But what really surprises me, is something he says mixed in with what he says about Mr. Kline.

"We also want to remember Mr. Foster in a special way. Mr. Foster lost his son, Chad, in the Korean War." There are whispers of surprise — a sort of ripple, especially from our class. *We didn't know.* But I remember those times when he got all choky. I look at Mr. Foster. His head is bowed.

I keep having the shivery-shakes and, the closer it gets to my turn to speak, the worse it gets. I don't know why I'm so jittery, since I have only a tiny part. Maybe because even that tiny part might make the veterans mad.

Now there's only one more part before mine. A bunch of little kids go up front and sing *Over Hill, Over Dale*. They sing as loud as they can and bang on drums. My heart hammers with the beating drums. The little kids have big smiles. It's confusing, because I have a big sadness, but some parts of the program feel almost happy. These smiling kids probably think war is the most wonderful thing. Or maybe they just like banging on drums. One good thing about this song, it lets me shake and wiggle and tap my feet, which I need to do because of my shivery-shakes. They're almost finished. My heart hammers harder. Now they're going back to their seats.

"Rose Penner will make a closing statement," says Mr. Bain.

My legs feel like rubber and my throat is dry as I go up front.

18

Speak From My Heart

I hold up a crane. The crane is trembling. I'm trembling. "Some of us made these ... um ... peace cranes to give out to you when you leave, because we hope that someday there will be no more wars."

I start to go back to my seat, but something doesn't feel right. *I don't feel finished.* I get only as far as the side of the stage. I stop. *One sentence is not enough!* I have to tell them *why* the crane is a symbol of peace. Maybe just one more sentence — or two. I turn at the side of the stage to face the audience.

"Uh ... there was this girl, Sadako, in Hiroshima, who died last year because of the atom-bomb disease." I say this all in a big rush because Mr. Foster is frowning at me. I look away from him. I can't just stop in the middle. "When she died, she was only twelve years old — almost the same age as I am. And I don't understand about the bomb ..."

There is some rustling and shuffling from the audience. Mr. Foster is shaking his head, 'no.' I don't know what to do. I glance at the veterans, who are probably boiling mad at me, too. But one face smiles back at me. I am so surprised that tears spring to my eyes. *That's gotta be Mr. Lambert.* He gives a little nod. I feel braver. "... I don't understand about the bomb because of Sadako, and the thousands of others who died, and ... that makes me befuddled in my mind about war." *Oh, I'm messing this up.* I shouldn't have said it *that* way. A few people laugh, but the laughing sounds nervous. My legs start to tremble. If I'd known I was going to say more than one sentence, I would have planned it all out.

Mr. Bain walks towards me. "Rose, maybe now isn't the time ..."

"Let her speak," says Probably-Mr. Lambert in a really big voice. "I, for one, want to hear what this brave young woman has to say."

Mr. Bain stops.

Brave young woman. I feel all sobby, but don't let the sobs out, because I'm a brave young woman. I bite my bottom lip.

It is completely quiet. Not a whisper or a ripple.

I look at Mr. Lambert. I feel sure it's him. Again he smiles and nods. I take a deep breath. I move back to the middle of the stage. Now what? *Speak from my heart.*

"Um ... I think you are all very brave for being in the war. I want to be brave, too. I want to work for freedom and democracy, too. But because of my religion, I didn't even know whether to take a poppy, when Tom passed them out. I took a poppy because I am so sorry about all the brave soldiers who died and got injured."

I look right at Mr. Foster. "I took a poppy because I'm so sorry your son, Chad, died." My voice gets wobbly. Mr. Foster looks down. It's really quiet now. I think they're actually listening.

I look right at Judy. "I took a poppy because of your papa. I can't even imagine how it would feel if *my* papa had died." Judy's mamma dabs at her eyes.

"And I took a poppy because of all the people who died because of Hitler ... and the bomb. I ... uh ... don't know yet what I'm going to do to be brave — something different than war — because ..." *Dare I say what's in my head?* "... because my religion believes ... and I believe — that ... war just makes more war." A murmur ripples through the room. A veteran behind me clears his throat in an angry way.

Mr. Bain walks towards me again. "We really have to bring this to a close."

"Let her finish!" Again Probably-Mr. Lambert's big voice. "Today we heard a lot about freedom and democracy, including Rose's wish to join in this effort. Whether or not we agree with her, what kind of freedom and democracy would deny her a voice?"

It gets almost quiet again, but there are a few rustly sounds.

And, wonder of wonders, all at once Sandra is standing beside me. I'm so surprised that I throw my arms around her, right in front of everybody. Again there is some nervous laughing. Sandra's eyes are big and her face is flushed, but she gives me a thin smile. "Finish telling about Sadako," she whispers into my ear. She slips her hand into mine.

I hear coughs and throat clearing. I know I better finish in a hurry. I ignore my hammering heart and my butterfly belly. "I have to finish telling you about Sadako, who died from radiation." I start rushing my words together again. "A Japanese legend says that if a sick person folds one thousand paper cranes, she will get well." I don't dare look at Mr. Foster. "Sadako started folding cranes, but she died before she got to a thousand." Mr. Bain is shuffling from one foot to the other. I rush my words even faster. "A statue is being built in Hiroshima of Sadako holding a paper crane. The statue is to remember Sadako and all the children who died." Uh-oh, Mr. Bain is coming closer. "Andthat'swhycranesaresymbolsofpeace." Everyone laughs, I guess because of my run-together words. My face is hot and my heart is thumpity-bumping, but I feel *so* good.

As Sandra and I go back to our seats, one woman stands up and claps. My eyes fill up. She stands there all by herself clapping. Now *that* is brave. Just one person clapping. Then Mr. Lambert gets up ... then someone else. Three people standing.

"You were so brave," I tell Sandra right after the assembly. "I mean, standing beside me. And it helped me be brave."

"I did it for you," she says. "And for Sadako ... and to help peace."

Judy, Sandra, and I hand out cranes as people leave. Oh, and Tom does too. "I'll help," he says and takes a whole bunch. "What you said took a lot of guts." He smiles at me.

"You said the *Flanders Fields* poem really well," I say.

"Tom," says Sandra, "I need one of those poppies." He grins and gives her one.

Cindy stands nearby, kind of shifting from one foot to the other.

"Do you want to help pass out these cranes?" I ask.

"I would, but ... my papa ..." She looks at the veteran with the run-together eyebrow. So that one really is her papa.

"It's okay," I say. "You don't have to help."

But she straightens up, marches over, and takes some cranes. "I'll help."

I grin at her. All at once I feel so crazy happy.

Cindy's papa sees Cindy take the cranes and hurries to where we are standing. He glares at me and hisses, "Little girl, you haven't the slightest idea about the complications that make war *absolutely* necessary."

I won't let him take away the glad feeling I have. I won't let *anyone* take it away. Not even that old Uncle Sam guy who is just coming past. I would bet that he's mad too. But he smiles at me. "May there be no more wars." I give him the biggest grin ever, and the best crane in the whole pile.

A few people won't take a crane and walk

right past, but most folks smile and say thank you. Some say I am brave. The woman who stood up all alone and clapped takes my hand and says, "That was very moving. You have spunk." *Spunk!*

"Thank you for standing up. That took ... um ... spunk, too." She laughs.

And here comes the guy who is probably Mr. Lambert. He looks right into my eyes. "It is a pleasure to meet you, Rose." He shakes my hand. "I am Mr. Lambert."

Suddenly I feel shy. I look down at first, but then look at him. "Thank you for ... you know ... making them let me speak." He just smiles at me.

* * *

Mr. Lambert and I sit on the school steps. He is holding a crane. He got one of the crooked, lop-sided ones. He's wearing jeans and a white shirt. His eyes are kind. He reminds me a bit of Papa. Mr. Lambert looks just ... ordinary. Yet he had such a strong voice at the assembly — such a big voice from someone so ordinary.

"What you said today took courage," he says.

"You, too," I say. "Maybe now all the other veterans are mad at you."

"Won't be the first time I've ruffled a few feathers." Then he says, "You Mennonites have something important to teach the rest of the world about peaceful ways of solving problems."

I am surprised. "Most folks around here don't think so," I say.

"'Most folks aren't always right."

I think about his words. Then I ask, "Mr. Lambert, are you really confused about war?"

"Yes, I am." Then, just for a second, his sad eyes turn twinkly. "War makes me so smad."

We both laugh.

"I'm smad, all right," he says. Now he does sound really smad. "I have some terrible pictures in my mind that haunt me to this day. I especially remember one young soldier, who didn't seem much older than that young lad who recited *In Flanders Fields*. The soldier was shot and I carried him from the battlefield. He died in my arms. It almost feels like I've been carrying him every day of my life since then." He stops and runs his hand through his hair. "The war is never really over for a veteran. It wasn't over for Mr. Kline ... so he ended it ... in his own way. And the war isn't over for me, because of the memories."

I don't know what to say, so I don't say anything.

He looks at me and smiles a sad smile. "You know, Rose, I wish I knew the answers to the hard questions about war. They sent us off with bands and banners, and we went marching off with pride and high hopes. But the reality was blood, guts, and misery. Ah, what am I saying to someone of your tender age?"

"I like it when grown-ups talk to me about real stuff."

He nods. "I can see that about you."

"Mr. Lambert, I have a big question, but I don't know how to ask it."

"Just ask it straight out."

"Um ... have you changed your mind from when you were younger? If you had to do it over again, would you go to war?"

He sighs. He doesn't say anything for a long time — stares into the distance. "That's a tough one, Rose, but ... probably, even though I have some hard questions about war."

"Oh." My voice is really quiet, disappointed.

"You're not a young woman I'd want to lie to. Sometimes an enemy does something so ... terrible, that ... that I don't know a way, other than war, of stopping them, though I hope I'm wrong. Sometimes the victims of our enemies need our help — like the Jews who were killed by Hitler. Sometimes a soldier saves a greater number of lives by taking some lives."

Lots of thoughts are buzzing around in my head, like *when the bomb was dropped on Hiroshima, that took thousands of lives.* But I say only one thing out loud. "Is there another way to help the victims of our enemies?"

He looks right into my eyes. "Rose, I hope you find a way."

How can I find a way? Mr. Lambert's words remind me of something he said in his letter. "Do you really think I'll do something important in the world?" I ask. I peek at him, shy again. Maybe asking that is boastful.

He looks surprised. "Why, Rose, you're already doing something important in the world. Didn't you know?"

"I am?"

"Of course — questioning an old guy like me, the cranes," — he holds up his lopsided crane — "standing up today and speaking up to those military folks. That took a *tremendous* amount of courage." He stares into the distance some more, then talks again in a far-away voice. "Soldiers say they die for 'freedom' and 'democracy' and 'justice.' But what if all that fighting serves no purpose whatsoever? I'd hate to think so." He looks so sad. "Yes, Rose ..." He gives me a half smile. "I'm befuddled in my mind too."

We sit quietly for a long time, both wondering about the why of things, especially the why of war. A meadowlark sings into the silence. *The larks still bravely singing, fly...*

"Mr. Lambert," I say finally.

"Yes."

"Tell me about your dog Spot."

"Oh, ho!" He laughs. I'm glad I made him laugh. "Now, Spot, he was some special pooch ..."

19

A Piece of Forever

I sit on our porch steps. I notice a tiny plant growing right through a crack in the cement sidewalk in front of me. It reminds me of Daniel asking whether flowers could grow through stone. It makes me smile.

I don't sit in Grandmother Oak's branches quite as much as I used to. I can think forever thoughts anywhere. I'm thinking about peace and war. About being alive and being dead. About Judy's papa. About Sadako. About yesterday's Veterans Day assembly. About Mr. Lambert. I wonder if it could really happen that there would be no more wars. Maybe someday. Maybe not. I sigh. But it doesn't mean we shouldn't try.

And all the while, the words of the *Flanders Fields* poem roll over and over in my head.

"In Flanders Fields the poppies blow
Between the crosses row on row ..."

Daniel pops out from under the steps. "What are fwanders fee-odes? And what are poppies?" I had hardly realized I was saying the poem out loud.

"Flanders Fields are ... um ... graveyards."

"With dead peep-o?" He gets that scrunchy-faced, sad look. Well, what do I expect? He gets sad when a sparrow dies.

"Uh-huh." I don't tell him that the graveyards are for soldiers. I don't want to get into a long conversation about hard-to-explain things. "And poppies are beautiful red flowers."

"Oh. Say those words again, Rose, about fwanders fee-odes."

"In Flanders Fields the poppies blow
Between the crosses, row on row ..."

He tilts his head to one side, then gets a knowing look. "O-o-oh! The dead peep-o hewped the poppies grow." He thinks about this for a couple of seconds, then adds, "I guess they didn't have coffin boxes."

Daniel runs off to the garden. I'm glad to be alone again. I haven't finished my wonder-thoughts. I wonder what I can do to help peace — I mean, when I grow up, though Mr. Lambert said I'm doing something already. Whatever I do, I have to be just as brave as the soldiers. *We must be willing to die for what we believe, but we must never kill for what we believe.*

Being brave. I guess I was brave yesterday, all right. Mr. Lambert sure was brave, speaking up like that, in front of all those other veterans. Soldiers are brave, for going to war. And Papa was brave for *not* going to war, and standing up for what he believed, even though other guys made fun of him. And that woman, yesterday, who stood up all by herself and clapped. And Sandra coming to stand beside me. That made me feel so happy. And also Cindy, who helped hand out the cranes, even though it made her papa mad. Daniel is *for sure* brave — wanting to save every single animal in the whole world. And Aunt

157

Bette, for ... well, for just being Aunt Bette, even though lots of people don't like the way she is. And Zippy is getting braver all the time, just like Dancer got brave.

I feel — I don't know — *quiet* inside myself right now. I look around at the real-live pictures of what's going on.

Daniel squatting in the dried-up November garden, all hunched, the way I see him so often. Probably looking at some worm or bug.

Papa coming from the barn with a frothing pail of milk.

Stinker trotting after him, tail held high.

Papa stopping to talk to Daniel. Setting down the milk. Crouching to look at whatever Daniel's looking at.

Stinker putting her front paws over the milk pail and lapping it up.

Me, chuckling, but not doing anything to stop Stinker from drinking the milk.

Daniel pointing at Stinker and laughing.

Papa shooing and scolding Stinker, but hardly like he means it. Actually, he's smiling.

Zippy sitting near me, but not on my lap. Maybe someday. Maybe not. But he comes closer every day, so I can hope.

Mamma coming outside, humming. *Mairzy doats.* I smile. "Mamma, swing your hips, like Elvis." She gives her hips a little jiggle. I burst out laughing. Even hip-jiggling is brave — when you're not used to it.

Right now, this is my piece of forever.

Author Note

Like Rose, I grew up in a Mennonite community that believed in nonviolent ways of solving problems. And like Rose, I remember being called "chicken" because our people didn't go to war. We were conscientious objectors, a term used for those who have a conscience against war. Many found other ways of serving, such as working for Civilian Public Service (CPS) which was active during World War II. Conscientious objectors can now apply to do alternative service, which offers peace-building projects all over the world. Mennonite Central Committee (MCC) is one organization which sponsors such projects. I, myself, worked through MCC as a day-camp leader with children in Chicago's inner city, and as an inner-city community worker in Hamilton, Ontario.

Mennonites follow the teachings of Jesus, as do other Christian groups. Also they believe in adult baptism. Instead of being baptized as babies, each person chooses to be baptized when he or she is old enough to make this decision. Many Mennonites believe in a simple life, though lifestyles vary among the many groups. Few are as strict as in earlier times, though some still avoid modern things and dress plainly. Though some early Mennonites stayed apart from the rest of the world, today many are right smack in the middle of things, believing it is best to work where there is a need. For example, Mennonites have worked with other groups to form an organization called Christian Peacemaker Teams (CPT). This organization sends trained peacemakers to troubled and war-torn places all over the world.

I still believe in solving problems non-violently. And I still struggle with how to do this, because it isn't easy, of course. Yet, I feel that a peaceful solution is the only kind that lasts.

To learn more about Mennonites and their beliefs, visit the following website: www.thirdway .com/menno.

It is important to recognize that other groups, and many individuals — not only Mennonites — are conscientious objectors. Thousands, from all races and religions, believe in solving problems in ways other than war.

Laurel Dee Gugler

Acknowledgements

The Ontario Arts Council offered assistance for this book through their Writers' Reserve granting program. I am deeply grateful.

Thank you, also, to the many readers, in the early stages, who gave valuable input. These included Susan Chapman, Rebecca Upjohn-Snyder, Thereza Dos Santos, Judy Gilbert, Carol Leigh Wehking, Glenna Janzen, Harriet Xanthakos, and Jocelyn LoSole-Stringer. Jocelyn's observations were especially valuable in providing a pre-teen point of view.

Later editorial assistance was invaluable. This included the insightful help of Faye Smailes, Allison McDonald, Anne Laurel Carter, and Kat Mototsune, whose expert observations helped profoundly to shape the book and tie the various strands together.

In addition, research assistance was provided by Duane Johnson and Dale Weishaar. And during the crucial last stages, computer help was provided by Dwain Swick, and writing space by Clare Goering.

Most of all, I am grateful to my ancestors who left a rich heritage, which encourages me to look for peaceful solutions to difficult problems.

Apologies to those who have been inadvertently omitted from these acknowledgements.

Laurel Dee Gugler

Sources

Children of the Paper Crane by Masamoto Nasu (translated by Elizabeth W. Baldwin, Steven L. Leeper, and Kyoko Yoshida, An East Gate book, New York, London: 1991) was an important resource. References to the *Hokkaido Shimbun* is from p. 147 of *Children of the Paper Crane*, and references to the *Chugoku Shimbun* is from p. 176.

Much of the information from Chapter 16 is taken from the book *Hiroshima, The Story of the First Atom Bomb*, by Clive A. Lawton (Candlewick Press, Cambridge, Massachusetts: 2004).